Bedroom GANGSTA

A NOVEL BY BEST SELLING AUTHOR
J. TREMBLE

Life Changing Books in conjunction with Power Play Media
Published by Life Changing Books
P.O. Box 423 Brandywine, MD 20613

Library of Congress Cataloging-in-Publication Data;

www.lifechangingbooks.net
13 Digit: 978-1934230286
10 Digit: 1-9344230282

Acknowledgements

First I would like to thank my loving family, my loyal friends and my faithful readers for all the support, advice and encouragement that everyone provided me while I worked on this novel. It seems like only yesterday when I took out a pencil and comprehension tablet as I sat at my extended families house in Connecticut during Thanksgiving. It was just a way to occupy my time as the women conversed in the kitchen and all the football games had been completed. I penned Secrets of a Housewife and my career of being an author began. Now, as I release my fifth novel, I still have many of the same people in my corner helping me in all areas of the writing process.

To my number one fan, my mother. I'm so glad to see how proud you are of me in all aspects of my life. The way you call me at any time to meet you somewhere to sign a book, meet a fan or just to tell me that you're out working at getting me sales. I love you so much for that. It's time to fill that oversized pocket book and hit the beauty salons, the hand dance clubs and senior citizen bus trips all over again.

I've changed schools since my first novel, but I still must thank the staff at Benjamin Stoddert, Region 1, Suitland Elementary and now my new home at Carmody Hills Elementary for giving me feedback on chapters, purchasing my novels and helping me get it out to the masses. All that you do is truly appreciated. Special thanks to Michelle Lewis, Lisa Sutton, Jerome Davis, Momma and Daughter Singletary's, Ms. Williams, Ms. McMillian, Byron Curry, Mr. Walker, Ms. White, Ms. Wynn, the cafeteria staff, the custodial staff and all the other staff that contributed to this finished product.

I also want to thank those special members who continue to be a part of my life. My second family, Rough Riders Flag Football Team. You guys work so hard to make sure that everyone knows that my books are out and how they can get them even if that means taking them yourselves. To Coach Gerald, Kurt, Jamaal, Charmin, Coach Dave, Derrick, Titus, Nardy, Big Ray, Ray Lite, Trina, Al, Go-Go, Speedy, Marlin, No-No, Rudy, Choo, all three Darryl's, Jerell, Kevin, little Dave, Wayne, Troy, Big and little Chris, Terry, Keith, Donte, Randy, Jermaine, Bootsy, Gina, Reece, Reds and all those past and future team-mates I didn't mention. Your support is greatly appreciated.

To my LCB family, it's a honor to have authors with such amazing titles working alongside of me for Life Changing Books. Because of talented writer's such as Azarel, Danette Majatte, Tonya Ridley, Tiphani, Mike Warren, C.J. Hudson, Miss KP, Jackie D, Kendall Banks, Carla Pennington, VegasClarke, Capone & all the other authors putting out bestselling books, you're the reason why I continue to write. I don't want to let you down, so I work to impress you first. Keep doing your thing and I'll be in your corner the same way you stay in mine.

To all the distributors who sell my novel(s) all around the world, I want to thank you. Especially the independent African American book stores that struggle through the hard times keeping your doors open so authors like myself can come and mingle with our readers both novice and veteran. You are the foundation to making sure African American writer's have a place to showcase our talents whether first time or seasoned.

I would like to thank the most important person of the entire writing and publishing process. Leslie Allen, I will never let a moment go by without expressing my gratitude for everything that you do to help me. It begins from the very moment I get an idea about a story, moves to the development of a title, the outline, then the editing process with your RED pen once I turn the manuscript in, transitions to one chapter at a time, and ends with a novel that brings enjoyment to readers. It may be a slight exaggeration if I mentioned that this book would not have been possible without you, but it's an absolute fact. Thanks for ALL THAT YOU DO!!!!

To my publisher Azarel, you found the courage to take a chance in a new writer and gave me a home in LCB. Whenever I needed anything from you, you've always found the time to provide me with advice whether business or personal. I appreciate that we have a mutual respect for each other and that I am more than just an employee, with that I can say that you are a friend. You keep having faith in me and I will continue to create books you are proud to add to the LCB collection.

Lastly, to all the readers out there reading my work, thank you. Writers would be nothing if not for you. The way you form book clubs, discuss our work in great detail, and open your homes to share both positive or negative feedback is amazing. The many nights you keep the little light on so you can read just one more page that turns into just one more chapter and ends with I have to know the ending is truly commendable. Thank you for all your comments on Amazon, lifechangingbooks.net and other social media outlets to make sure other readers know that we exist and it is worth their time to check us out. You keep this train of literature moving. Don't slow down now, thank you!!

Peace,
The King of Erotica,
J. Tremble

Chapter One

"Ahh…yes," Bryce moaned between a constant flow of heavy breathing.

Not fully awake, he slowly rolled from side to side as his toes began curling from the enjoyable sensation rushing up and down his body. Bryce rubbed the blurriness from his eyes while little sounds of soft sighs echoed in his head. As his vision started to clear up, he noticed his wife, Seven on her knees sliding her tongue up his thick, circumsized dick. With all the shit on his mind lately, Bryce really didn't want to engage in any sexual contact. He even wanted to reach down and push Seven off of him, but the warmth of her mouth and softness of her lips made him submit to their regular morning routine.

At that point Bryce smiled, then started watching her movements, enjoying Seven's oral skills. He loved how his wife's long, blonde streaked hair hung over her face as her tongue did several acrobatic moves. Seven knew how much Bryce loved to watch her mouth work his dick, so she flicked her hair over her shoulder to give him a clear view. She then glanced up to lock eyes with her man just to make sure he was watching.

Great minds think alike, Bryce thought as Seven massaged his shaft a couple of times, then played magician by making three-fourths of his dick, disappear inside her mouth.

Bryce closed his eyes and clutched the sheets with both of his hands as Seven worked her magic. However, right before the moment of climax, she quickly released him from her warm jaws. Frantically, he tried to force her mouth back down on his pulsating penis so he could finish his orgasm. When Bryce finally opened his eyes, he watched as she crawled up his legs, taking position to ride him.

"It's too early in the morning for you to be playing games. I'm ready to explode and your mouth was a good place to catch it," Bryce said.

"I want us to cum together," Seven whispered.

"What's wrong baby? Don't you need your morning protein? You know an ounce of my nut keeps the pimples away."

Ignoring her husband's joke, Seven looked over at the alarm clock. The glowing 6:35 a.m. made her quickly cut off communication before sliding her dripping pussy down his shaft. Not only did they have an hour before both of them left for their meaningless jobs, Seven needed a good orgasm to start off her day like most people needed Starbucks coffee. She didn't want to waste any more time.

Seven's body shook as Bryce's oversized dick rubbed against her entire womb. She laughed, reflecting back to the first time she saw his enormous manhood, thinking there was no way in hell she would be able to take it all in. Even though it seemed as if his dick touched his knee cap, it wasn't even fully erect.

Bryce quickly interrupted Seven's flashback as he smacked her left ass cheek to get her moving. Obviously Bryce wanted Seven to go from the slow 'ride the pony' pace, to the speed of a cowgirl from a bronco riding competition.

"So, is that how we're rolling this morning?" Seven asked, sliding her hands over his toned chest.

"Yeah, I need you to crank it up to triple X mode. We both have to go to work." Bryce stared into her cinnamon colored eyes. "Besides, don't you wanna get rough?"

"As a matter of fact, I do," Seven said, wrapping her hands around Bryce's neck before applying pressure. "Now…talk that shit!"

Thinking a good banging would cut the game short, Bryce bounced her body up and down on his pole. However, once he realized the rough pounding still didn't release her grip, he started twisting his head back and forth, hoping that would signal Seven to let go. He even tried to lift up off of the bed, but that didn't work either.

"Don't you fucking move. I told you that I wanted to get rough," Seven said pushing him back on the bed and applying more pressure.

It wasn't long before Bryce's eyes filled with water and he really appeared to be choking. At that point, Seven finally released her grip and placed them on her thick hips. She smiled…he didn't.

"What the hell is your problem?" Bryce asked as he gasped for air.

"I remember when you used to love S&M in the morning. I'm so disappointed," Seven responded.

"I do, but you be taking that shit too far sometimes," Bryce said, rubbing his neck.

Seven shook her head. "Stop whining. People who engage in S&M don't worry about if something hurts or not."

Feeling the need to show her who the man of the house was, Bryce grabbed his wife's waist with both arms and pulled her hour glass figure down onto his twelve and a half inches. As Bryce's dick seemed embedded into Seven's pussy, suddenly his tool hit that spot inside her walls that always sent Seven's eyes rolling to the back of her head. Her body was overcome with sensations from head to toe, while Bryce continued to grind against that once hidden spot. It wasn't long before Seven started speaking a foreign language. She was on the verge of exploding when Bryce pushed her off and started to laugh.

"You don't deserve to cum," he said, sliding up the bed and resting against the headboard.

"Oh, that shit was wrong on so many levels. You better not leave me hanging or I swear to God I'll Al Green your ass with some hot grits!" Seven shouted.

"Damn, calm down. I was just fucking with you. Besides, didn't your ass just leave me hanging when I was about to bust a nut?"

"So, are you on some get back type shit?" Seven asked. Bryce knew how irritated she became when he played around during their sex sessions.

"No. I just didn't want you to experience your usual orgasm. I mean, we haven't had a nice, calm a.m. love making encounter in quite some time," Bryce replied.

"Please don't tell me you're trying to switch shit up now because I'm not really into boring ass Susie homemaker sex."

"Nothing has changed with me. I still love rough, heated sex, but I just wanted something different this time."

"Oh, I'm sorry. Maybe I need to ask you what you're in the mood for before we get started since my needs don't matter anymore," Seven said sarcastically. She could no longer sit idle listening to Bryce talk any longer. Not to mention, he was killing her mood. "You know what…just forget it."

Realizing that things were about to go the wrong way, Bryce rushed toward Seven and started kissing her passionately. Moments later his shrinking shaft quickly stood straight up poking Seven in her inner left thigh. No matter what the situation was, Bryce had no control over his sexual emotions when it came to Seven. He longed for her smell, craved her touch and yearned to feel her body in his arms.

Bryce rolled Seven over onto her back and began massaging her mango sized breasts and shoulders. Bryce then slid between Seven's smooth, chiseled caramel legs and rubbed his pulsating penis against her protruding clit. They both moaned as Bryce slowly eased his dick back inside her, pausing just long enough to tickle her clit with his middle finger. Bryce went right back to Seven's spot once his dick was fully inserted. He raised her legs, locked them with his shoulders and rotated his hips until she let out a piercing scream.

Bryce clutched her voluptuous ass with both hands. He arched his back and pounded with all his might for a few seconds, then chased it with a circular grind. He kept this up until one of Seven's legs slid off his shoulder down to the bed. At that point, Bryce used this opportunity to roll her over into another position. He held the one leg up in the air and maneuvered his body so their bodies formed a set of geometrical parallel lines.

Now, with his dick entering her pussy at an angle, Seven's spot was fully exposed. Bryce used his strong muscular arms to lift her off of the bed and bang even faster. Bryce watched as his wife bit her lower lip and clutched her hands into a fist. He chuckled as they began shaking uncontrollably.

"Baby, I love you so much," Bryce moaned.

"I love you, too. Please don't stop this time. I'm almost there…I'm almost there," Seven cried out.

"Damn, this pussy is so good. I'm about to cum," Bryce softly confessed.

"Don't stop. Right there baby, that's the spot."

"Yes…oh, yes, baby," Bryce said.

It appeared as if their moans and screams of reaching a climax together woke up the sun. It's warming rays crept across the bedroom from the window and filled the room with an orange colored light. Now, Bryce could see the emotions on Seven's beautiful face. As she dug her hands into the sheets, Bryce watched as her face tightened. Her breathing was short and quick. He knew she was experiencing a powerful orgasm.

Bryce tried to concentrate. He wanted to cum at the very exact moment.

"Yes!" Seven screamed out as louder screams of ecstasy soon followed.

Bryce began to move his body faster to hurry his orgasm. "Yes, baby, hold on for a few more seconds so I can join you," he said as his toes curled. "I'm getting ready to cum."

"Don't cum in me. Shoot it on my stomach," Seven insisted in a stern voice.

Suddenly, Bryce looked down at his wife with an '*are you serious*' look on his face. He was extremely confused, but a sudden banging on their front door made him not want to spend that moment trying to figure out her reasoning. Bryce ignored the knocking and kept stroking with long deep thrusts until his nut was at the tip of his dick. Just when Bryce was ready to unload, Seven maneuvered her body so his dick would fall out.

"Why the hell did you do that?" Bryce yelled.

"Don't you hear that banging?" Seven asked.

From the way Seven was acting Bryce could tell that she'd already came. "So what. Whoever it is can come back. You got yours, now I need to get mine." Bryce tried feverishly to ram his shaft back into Seven, but she twisted her body so he couldn't enter. "What are you doing? Are you acting like this just so I won't cum inside you?" he questioned.

As he thought about it, Seven never wanted him to cum inside of her anymore. There always seemed to be some type of excuse.

"Don't be silly. I just want you to get the damn door. Aren't you concerned why somebody is banging like that at this time of morning?" Seven replied.

Bryce used his knees to keep Seven's legs open. He continued to flick his dick against her clitoris, but Seven repeatedly prevented him from inserting it. Finally, Bryce became disgusted and stopped.

Seconds later, another barrage of hard knocks echoed from the front door of their little one bedroom apartment. When Bryce looked over to see that it was 7:00 a.m., his anger seemed to increase. They both assumed it was their drunk neighbor Moochie. She was probably upset that their loud love making woke her up again since she wasn't known to get up before noon.

Bryce crawled off Seven, gave her a long stare still wondering why she told him not to cum inside her, then turned to go answer the door. His long dick swung as he walked out of the room while Seven teased him by sticking two of her fingers into her dripping pussy.

Bryce watched as Seven opened her legs then slowly massaged her clit. Seven used her other hand to push up her breast to position it so her tongue could tickle her nipple. Her moans began to make Bryce's dick point like an arrow on a compass. When Seven realized that Bryce was hypnotized by her actions, she quickly slid another finger inside her juicy paradise. Seven then pressed her feet into the mattress and lifted her ass up into the air showing her husband that she was still flexible just like when they met three years ago.

As the knocking continued, all Bryce could do was shake his head and smile. Seven was such a tease…always had been, but he loved that about her. It actually turned him on most of the time. Seconds later, Bryce stopped and snatched a towel from the bathroom before continuing to the door.

If this is Moochie at my door, I'ma kill her ass for fucking up my nut, Bryce thought.

The knocks were getting louder with each step he took. When Bryce finally made it to the door, he looked through the peep hole to find his big, black over-weight landlord standing there with a disgusted look on her face.

Shit, I don't have the rent money yet, Bryce thought.

He hesitated for a minute, contemplating if he should open the door or not, but knew she wasn't going away. Against his better judgment, Bryce jerked the door open.

"Why the hell do we have to go through this shit every time I need my fuckin' rent money?" the landlord boasted.

BEDROOM GANGSTA

8

Chapter Two

"Do you know what time it is?" Bryce asked staring at the landlord's curly mustache. He'd never seen a woman who resembled a man as much as she did.

"You damn right I know what time it is. If your punk ass was a good tenant and gave me my rent money on time instead of duckin' me every month, I could be sleep right now," she said in her usual deep voice. With a cigarette lodged between her fingers, she took a quick pull, then blew smoke directly in his face.

Bryce waved the smoke away before looking back over his shoulder to see if Seven was behind him. He didn't want her to hear their conversation. "Can you keep your damn voice down, Ms. Manly? My wife is still trying to sleep."

"Who the hell are you talkin' to? My name is Medley, Phyllis Medley, not Manly muthafucka. And I know she's up already. The paint chippin' off my ceilin' and the constant bangin' of your damn headboard is a clear indication that she's awake."

Bryce hated that Ms. Medley lived directly under them. He also hated living in the Saint Roch area of New Orleans. Every other night there appeared to be a homicide on the news.

Bryce eased the door closed. He tried to cover his body by crossing his arms across his chest as he turned around. Feeling completely uncomfortable, the last thing Bryce wanted was for one of his neighbors to see him talking to Ms. Medley with just a towel on.

Ms. Medley's nipples hardened as her eyes traced Bryce's six foot three milk chocolate frame. With a bald head and a neatly trimmed goatee, he reminded her so much of the actor D.B. Woodside. Bryce turned around to see Ms. Medley's eyes staring downward. It was then when he realized that a portion of his dick was hanging out.

"So, what's up?" Bryce asked repositioning the towel.

It took a second or two for Ms. Medley to focus. "Stop playin' dumb. You know damn well *what's up*. Where's my money? I need to see you countin' out some dead presidents in my palm. I'm not runnin' a fuckin' shelter!" she shouted.

"Please Ms. Manly, I…"

"Didn't I tell you to stop callin' me that shit?"

Bryce was so used to calling her that behind closed doors, it was hard to get it right. "Oh. I'm sorry, Ms. Medley. Listen, I need a little more time. I promise to have your money by the end of the month," Bryce replied.

She chuckled. "Are you stupid? Rent is due on the first, and today is the 10th. Your ass is already late and you have the nerve to ask me to wait even longer. By that time you'll need to pay me for another month."

"Yeah, I know but…" Bryce tried to say.

"But nothin'. You got 'til five p.m. to get me my damn money or I'ma call the police and tell 'em your ass is trespassin'. Better yet I might just call my son down here. Him and his boys will get yo' ass out of here. Either way, you gotta go."

Even though Ms. Medley owned the property, it was her gang affiliated son who enforced all the rules.

"I'm just tryin' to figure out if you and your wife both work, why the hell can't y'all pay my eight hundred dollars every month. Y'all better not be on that shit, cuz I don't want no drug addicts livin' here," Ms Medley continued.

Bryce stared at her fake Gucci print scarf and oil stained night gown. "We're not on drugs Ms. Medley."

She placed her hands on her wide hips. "Then what's the

problem?"

"Come on Ms. Medley. I'm waiting on some money to come in. How about giving me to the end of the week?" Bryce said, stepping a little closer.

She glanced down at Bryce's dick poking back out of the towel and smiled. "Okay, Mr. Deans, I'm gonna give you 'til the end of the week. But if I don't have my money, there won't be anymore extensions. I ain't got no problems puttin' you and your fuckin' drama queen wife out on the street. Just in case you haven't noticed, this ain't your average apartment complex. We don't go through the courts to get you out. We do it ourselves."

"I understand. Thank you Ms. Medley. I'll have the money by the end of the week. You won't have to worry about that," Bryce said turning to go back inside.

When Bryce felt a hard slap on his ass, he quickly turned back around which made the towel fall to the ground. Ms. Medley's eyebrows immediately rose.

"Have you lost your mind?" Bryce barked. He quickly snatched up the towel.

"Oh don't be shy. I'm sure your wife wouldn't mind sharing one day," Ms. Medley replied, before walking away and down the staircase. Her laugh could still be heard coming from the lower floor.

The thought of anybody fucking Ms. Medley made his stomach bubble. "I wouldn't even use the dick of my worst enemy to fuck that woman," Bryce said to himself.

After getting over the fact of her touching him, Bryce took a deep breath then turned the door knob. However, the door wouldn't open. He'd obviously forgotten to take the lock off before closing it. Bryce knew that Seven was probably going to be pissed since he'd taken so long to come back, so having to let him back in would surely irritate her even more. Trying to get himself prepared, Bryce knocked on the door several times before striking a sexy pose for Seven when she opened the door. He hoped his rock hard abs would at least make her smile, but his modeling session was useless. When Bryce heard Seven unlock the door but didn't bother to open it, he knew she'd walked away.

"Where's my sexy wife?" Bryce asked entering the apartment.

The slamming of the bathroom door quickly acknowledged Seven's whereabouts. Seconds later, she stormed out of the bathroom and walked toward the linen closet. After opening that door it wasn't long before she slammed that one too.

"I'm so fucking tired of never having the shit I need!" she shouted just before walking to their bedroom.

Bryce went to get a glass of orange juice hoping those few seconds would allow Seven to calm down before he went back in the bedroom. But the distant sound of other things being opened and shut with authority signaled that Seven had no intentions of easing up. Just as Bryce put his glass in the sink full of dirty dishes, Seven emerged from the bedroom with a stern and evil look.

"Do I look like fucking June Cleaver or Carol Brady to you?"

Bryce appeared confused. "Who is June Cleaver or Carol whatever? I'm lost."

"You watch TV Land at night. You know damn well who they are. They're the perfect stay at home wives who do nothing but have children, clean the house, cook and wash the fucking dishes like that glass you just put in the sink," Seven responded.

"How did we go from making passionate love to you cursing and slamming doors in less than twenty minutes?" Bryce asked.

"You must see stupid written on my forehead. I mean you're unbelievable. I just wanna know if you're serious because if you are, we don't have time for that shit," Seven said closing her robe.

Bryce wanted to respond, but Seven stormed off again. *She had to hear my conversation*, he thought rubbing his head.

When he walked into the bedroom, Seven was throwing shoes out their small, cramped walk-in closet. He heard her talking, but wasn't sure if the conversation was intended for his ears or just her own.

"I need to have my head examined. I was making really good money dancing at Temptations. I had the hottest set out of all them other bitches. I mean both pro and street ballers used to shower me with money every night." Seven flung a shoe so hard that it broke a glass vase that was once filled with a dozen pink and white tiger lilies, a twenty-ninth birthday gift she'd gotten from Bryce just a month before.

"Man, that motherfucka really fooled me. Coming in there night after night making it rain like he was paid. I can't believe I fell for the bullshit," Seven continued to mumble.

"Are you talking to me?" Bryce asked.

"Does it look like I'm talking to you? When I'm talking to you, you'll know it," Seven fired back.

As bad as Bryce wanted to respond, he had no rebuttal. When he thought about it, everything Seven said was completely true, and he actually felt bad about it. Looking back to when they first met, Bryce was completely infatuated the first time he saw Seven perform. The way she moved her thick thighs and apple shaped ass had every man in the club wanting to jerk off, and Bryce was no exception. Like all the other men, he had to have her, and from that point on, Bryce stopped at nothing to make the multiracial Creole beauty his girl. The fact that she was a stripper didn't bother him in the least. A bad bitch was all he saw and cared about.

During that time Bryce owned a profitable custom rim and detail shop. By providing the best in chrome rims, stereo systems, tint and hand wash jobs, Bryce did pretty well for himself. During that time he was able to shower Seven with stacks of money, keeping up with the rest of the local ballers. After finally convincing Seven to go out on a date with him, their once simple, stripper/customer affiliation soon blossomed into a full blown relationship. Bryce recalled the long sessions he spent with her in the private rooms of Temptations where he promised to give Seven everything her heart desired, including champagne wishes and diamond dreams. After their informal Vegas wedding everything was going according to plan until Bryce's father who helped him start and run the business died of a massive heart attack. Months after that, the economy crashed, which eventually caused Bryce to lose his shop. They'd been struggling ever since, which is why Bryce blamed himself and allowed Seven to vent every now and then.

Seven looked at the clock. "It's seven-thirty. Now, I'm gonna be late for work!"

Seven continued to yell out quick little rants, but Bryce still didn't reply. Instead, he walked into the bathroom and sat on the toilet. After he turned on the shower to let the water get hot, Bryce sat there rubbing his bald head. With Ms. Medley breathing down his back, and Seven pissed off, Bryce had no idea what he was gonna do.

Suddenly, Seven kicked the door open like an action hero. "Tell me again why you don't want me to go back to Temptations."

"Seven, please. Do we have to go over this shit again?"

"Yes, we do have to go over this shit again. Maybe this time you'll make sense."

"Because you're my wife and no wife of mine is gonna be dancing for money."

"When you met me I was dancing for money."

"Yeah, and you weren't my wife then either. Now that you are, I don't want a stripper as a wife," Bryce responded.

"So wait, I'm supposed to stay broke for the rest of my life with a damn mechanic."

Bryce looked at Seven with piercing eyes. "That was fucked up."

He hated when she threw his occupation up in his face. Once his shop closed, Bryce took a job as a mechanic just to make ends meet. His salary now wasn't even a fraction of what he used to make.

"Well, it's how I feel. I can't believe I fell for that shit you used to kick to me. You told me that I wouldn't have to work again because you were gonna provide me with everything I ever wanted. Now, I can't even think about what I might want because I never have what the fuck I need."

"What do you need?" Bryce asked standing up. He stared at the small mole on her left cheek.

"Before I even do a roll call of the shit I need, just answer one damn question for me. What happened to the fucking rent money?"

Bryce sighed. His suspicious were true. Seven had obviously overheard him and Ms. Medley talking. "Look, it was either pay the rent or pay your car note, buy groceries, and keep the fucking lights on," Bryce answered in a stern voice.

"That's my point exactly. We can barely do the basic shit around here so why would I even waste my time thinking about all the things I need! I could pay my own damn car note if I made more money!" Seven shouted then slammed the bathroom door.

Yanking the door back open, Bryce ran after her. "Look, I'm doing the best I can. Shit won't be like this forever. I just need a little time."

"A little more time. Bryce we've been struggling for the past two and a half years, and you still haven't gotten it together. If you let me go dance again, then I'll make the money we need and then some."

"You already have a job."

Seven chuckled. "Oh really. I'm a fucking shampoo assistant at a salon. The amount I make on my weekly check, I could make that shit in an hour working at the club."

Bryce held a serious expression. "Well, if you're not happy with that job, then go look for another one, but dancing for money is not gonna happen."

"I never wanted that damn job. It was your idea for me to do this shit so I could learn how to run my own salon. The salon you promised that you were gonna buy me three years ago when I said 'I do'!" Seven roared.

"I had no idea the economy was gonna hit rock bottom.

After Katrina I thought things were gonna get better. Not to mention, my dad was here one day and gone the next. He helped me run the place. Don't you remember me losing it when I found out he didn't have a life insurance policy? I had to pay for his funeral out of pocket. I couldn't even afford to keep his house, and you know how much that house meant to me." Bryce stopped to think about his mother, who died of Diabetes when he was twenty-one. With Seven's lack of support most times, he felt alone. "We just hit a bad patch, but we'll make it through. I need you to have faith in me baby." When Bryce tried to hug her, Seven pulled away.

"I'm trying, but I just don't know how much more of this shit I can handle. You have to understand, before I met you I'd been stripping for six years, so I'm not used to living like this." Seven looked around the room. "I mean look at this place. Everything is so fucking outdated in here. Something needs to happen for us because I have no intention on letting you take me down," Seven advised.

Bryce was getting ready to respond when he heard a horn beeping out front. When he walked over to the window, his boy Mitch's car was double parked in front of his apartment. "Shit. I haven't even taken a shower," Bryce said as he lifted up the window and stuck his head out. "I need about fifteen more minutes!"

"I'm gonna run to get some coffee. You better be ready when I get back!" Mitch yelled back.

"We'll finish this conversation when we get back home tonight," Bryce said to Seven after closing the window.

"If you didn't let the snatch man repossess your damn car you wouldn't need your boy to give you a ride every morning like a little child," Seven replied sarcastically.

"Well, if you would take me to work, I wouldn't need him to help me out."

"And waste my gas? Please. Mitch has two jobs. He can afford to ride your ass around town, I can't."

Bryce had already lost the battle for trying to bust an

early morning nut, then his landlord had threatened to kick him out on the street, and now Seven was dropping bombs on his ability to provide for her like a real man. He wanted to slap the shit out of her spoiled ass, but instead of catching a charge, he once again just walked away.

Chapter Three

By the time Mitch pulled back up to the apartment, Bryce was standing outside. Mitch noticed that Bryce looked as rundown as the two story building he was living in on Elysian Fields Avenue. The building had four small one bedroom apartments, with rusty bars covering the first floor windows, which were so dirty they appeared to be tinted.

"What up homie?" Mitch shouted as Bryce got in.

"Same shit, just a different color," Bryce replied. Even though he tried to disregard it, Seven's voice repeating the words, "like a little child," played over and over in his head.

"When the fuck are you getting another car? I'm tired of you hopping in my shit with that feel sorry for me, ball and chain bringing me down type attitude every day," Mitch said pulling off.

"Man, I can't even pay my rent on time. Getting a new car is nowhere near my thoughts. I'm fucked up on so many levels. My life seems to be spinning out of control," Bryce said hitting his fist against the dashboard.

"Nigga, have you lost your mind? I'll pull this muthafucka over and make you ride the damn bus if you beat on my shit again."

Bryce knew how much Mitch loved his new Cadillac Escalade.

"My bad dog, it's just that I really want to get my life moving. I'm ready to get Seven pregnant with two or three little shorties. The big house with the gated fence and a dog chasing the kids as they play in the yard is what I really want," Bryce said.

Mitch looked at his friend. "You playing right?"

"No, I'm not. Why the fuck you acting all surprised?"

Mitch laughed. "Slim, it is a surprise. Hell, I'm still shocked that you even married Seven in the first place. I mean she got that name for the seven different positions she could perform on stage. But I said okay, this nigga must've got turned out, so it'll only last a minute before he'll be filing for divorce. Now you talking kids and shit. Nigga, you can't be serious."

"You know what, pull over and let me out!" Bryce shouted.

"What for?"

"If you weren't my boy, I would knock your ass out for saying some shit like that about my wife. So, let me get the fuck out before this shit gets out of hand," Bryce replied.

"Nigga, stop faking. We're not in grade school, you gonna have to work to whip this two hundred and fifty-eight pounds."

With Mitch's tall stature, huge neck and massive hands, he was constantly mistaken as a football player.

"Well, keep Seven's name out your mouth because I'm not in the mood," Bryce warned.

"See, that's the day time soap opera shit I was talking about. I gotta constantly listen to you bitch and moan about all the fucked up shit in your life, and when I make a comment about it that you don't like, then you get a damn attitude."

"You my boy, but you gotta understand, that's my wife."

Mitch glanced over at Bryce. "I know who she is. I'm the reason you met her remember. Don't forget it was me who told you to come down to my new part time gig as a bartender down at the strip club. It was me who introduced you two when your scared ass didn't have the balls to. It was me who told you the nights she danced. I can't believe you're trying to be so defensive. I could still be in my fucking bed right now instead of driving you to work."

"Yeah, whatever. Just don't say nothing negative about my wife and we're cool," Bryce said leaning his head back against the seat.

"What?" Mitch responded.

"You heard me. You need to stop worrying about me and Seven and put your foot down on the pedal and get this truck moving. It's my turn to open up the shop and I was supposed to be there by eight. I'm late," Bryce advised.

"You're talking a lot of shit. You know nobody calls the shots in my ride. I wonder what time your punk ass will get to work if you have to use those old ass Air Force One's to get there."

Suddenly they both laughed. Ever since they met in the fifth grade, their arguments never lasted long before somebody said something funny. Bryce continued to think about their twenty year friendship as they made a left on North Claiborne Avenue. Mitch was definitely his nigga for life, and he appreciated his concern. It took Mitch about twenty minutes to drive to Dynamic Auto Salon, a small mom and pop garage located in the Riverbend neighborhood. Bryce wasn't surprised when he saw two cars already in the parking lot when they pulled up.

Bryce's face quickly lit up once the car stopped. "Good...people are here already. I hope it stays like this because I need to make some money. As long as I don't have to spend all day doing cheap ass oil changes, I'm good," he said getting out.

"Okay, master do you need me to pick you up after the shop closes?" Mitch asked teasing Bryce in his best southern accent.

"Real funny. I'll hit you on your cell and let you know."

"Cool."

"Excuse me, you're already late and I need to drop this car off and get to work. You can talk to your boyfriend later!" a pretty woman getting out of a Chrysler Sebring shouted.

Bryce glanced over in her direction with a crazy look on his face. "Sweetheart, I'm not sure what type of men you deal with, but you're barking up the wrong tree if you think either one of us are gay. So, let me open up the shop and get you on your way Miss Lady before I say something really unprofessional," Bryce replied. He gave Mitch a pound, then walked toward the shop doors.

It took a couple of minutes for Bryce to turn off the alarm, pull up the two garage bays and flip on the neon OPEN sign in the window. Moments later, Bryce opened and held the front door as he motioned for the woman to come inside.

As soon as she walked in, Bryce glanced over and noticed the small strawberry tattoo on the woman's right ankle. His eyes then ran up her toned legs to her protruding hips. A slight smile came over his face as he stopped at her firm breast poking out of her low cut shirt.

Once the woman realized Bryce was checking her out, she cleared her throat. It looked like she wanted to smile, but kept a stone like face instead. "Umm...I'm waiting."

Bryce walked behind the counter. "So, how can I help you?"

"I don't know why black people always gotta be on a different time schedule than every other race, but that shit is unacceptable. I hope this ain't gonna be a reflection of the work on my car," she scuffed.

"This has to be your first time at Dynamic Auto, but it won't be your last that I can promise."

"Are you saying that you're gonna rig my damn car so that it'll keep breaking down and I have to bring it back?" she questioned.

"No. I'm saying that I'll have your car done and running like new without costing you the price of a new one. I'm also saying that you'll bring it back for the regular maintenance cause I'm just that good," Bryce bragged. He handed her a clipboard with some papers attached. "By the way, I'm Bryce the mechanic and future owner of my own repair shop one day."

"Wow a grease monkey with a dream. Who'd ever think that was possible," she said taking the clipboard.

It took a second for her smart ass comment to register with Bryce. He rubbed his head and stared at the woman. *Damn, that's one bitter ass bitch. I bet some guy probably fucked her over*, he thought.

After all was said and done, the woman only wanted him to change her brake pads and rotors, along with an oil change, a job that wasn't gonna take long. Making most of his money from the hourly labor charges, Bryce was at least hoping for a suspension or transmission job.

"What time should I be back?" she asked.

"I have a couple of cars ahead of yours, so how about four this afternoon," Bryce answered handing her a business card and yellow work slip. "Call before you come."

"My name is Kayla," she said leaning over the counter to show more of her cleavage.

"Umm, nice to meet you Kayla," Bryce replied staring straight down her shirt.

"Is four the best you can do for me? Is there anything I can do? Oops…I mean you can do? I was hoping to get it during my lunch break so I can go home after work for a long, hot bath." She looked at the slip. "How much is it gonna be?"

Bryce began to imagine how she might look soaking in a tub filled with bubbles, then quickly snapped out of his trance. "The price depends on how long it's gonna take me to do everything. As far as the time, I'm already pushing it with four looking at all the cars ahead of yours. Next time, you need to make an appointment so you can get in and out early."

"Is this your private number on the card? Maybe next time you can come to my house and I won't need an appointment," Kayla replied in a sexy tone.

The bitch is either bipolar or she's trying to get this shit for free, Bryce thought. It wouldn't be the first time a woman had tried to exchange pussy for repair work.

"It's the shops number and I don't think my wife would like it if I worked on your car at your house unless she's there to supervise," Bryce responded.

Obviously pissed from Bryce's comment, Kayla stood up, then flung her long, black, curly hair over her shoulder. "You know what, I'll go somewhere else," she said before storming out.

She was moving so fast, she almost knocked the other mechanic Reggie down on her way out.

Reggie shook his head. "Damn, I see you're pissing women off already. As fine as that one was, I'm mad I wasn't here on time," he said entering the shop.

Bryce was finishing up his fourth car when his stomach started growling. He glanced over at the clock hanging on the far wall of the garage and realized it was quarter to one. It was lunch time already. When Bryce walked past the office, and headed toward the break room, he noticed his boss sitting behind his desk organizing some papers.

"Hey D, can I holler at you for a second?" Bryce asked sticking his head in.

"Sure, what's up?" Darrell said once Bryce walked in.

"I really need some more time added to my schedule. Right now you only have me working three to four days a week, but I could use more. I need to make some extra money."

Darrell dropped his head. "I wish I could, but business is real slow right now. I was hoping we'd pick back up since that other repair shop three blocks away closed down, but things are still pretty bad."

"D, I'm in a real bind right now. Can you at least give me an advance on my check? I gotta get some folks off my back."

Darrell pushed up his glasses. "Sorry Bryce. I just don't have the money to do that right now. Hell, Reggie just asked for the same thing yesterday, and I felt bad not being able to do it since he has a baby on the way. I just paid all the supply companies and the tax on the garage, so I need those checks to clear."

Bryce lowered his head. "Shit. I'm in a jam."

"Boy, please, you're only thirty-two. You don't know what a jam is. Wait until you get my age and you wake up with every part of your body aching and hair growing out of the craziest places."

Bryce laughed. "Come on Darrell, you need to work on a new speech. That's the same line you say all the time." He stared at Darrell's salt and pepper hair. "I mean I know your hairline has receded, but you look good to be fifty-six. So, anyway, listen, when can I become manager of this spot? I know I haven't been here as long as Reggie and the others, but I'm the best mechanic you got. Maybe then you'll give me more hours."

"Manager. I don't think so. Not when I just took a call from a customer complaining about the garage opening late and you making her feel uncomfortable by staring at her breasts," Darrell informed. "She even said you tried to touch her."

"What?" Bryce shouted.

"Yeah, she even threatened to call the police before I calmed her down. I told her to come back in and we would take fifty percent off her bill."

That crazy bitch, Bryce thought. "Look, I was running late today D, but I never tried to touch her. I wasn't staring at her breasts either. She's lying. You know that ain't me."

"Well, I can't have complaints like that, especially since you really are the best mechanic I have."

"I would never do something foul like that. I care about you and this place," Bryce added.

Darrell started laughing.

"It's not funny. I really care about how you think of me. I would never do anything to embarrass you or me," Bryce said rubbing his face.

"I wasn't laughing at you like that. I was just about to call you in here to see if you were interested in buying this garage, but I see that you're just as broke as the rest of us," Darrell said still laughing.

"What? You're selling the garage?"

"I have no choice. I told you that my wife was diagnosed with heart disease last year. Well, her last check up showed that her health is getting worse, so her doctor believes that we should relocate to Baltimore, Maryland so she can be close to a cardiac specialist at Johns Hopkins. I was thinking that it would take me about six months to get everything in order. I was hoping that you would be the one running this shop when I left," Darrell informed.

Bryce's eyes lit up like a Christmas tree. "Hell yeah, I would love to run it. Don't make a move without giving me a chance."

"If you're begging for your check in advance, how the hell are you gonna have the money to buy this garage?"

"Don't worry. I'm gonna figure something out. How much are you selling it for?"

"Well, it needs some work done, so I'm willing to let it go for eighty-five grand which is a steal. If you could at least come up with twenty percent, I would be willing to let you make payments until it's paid off," Darrell replied.

"Really?"

"Yeah, so that's around seventeen grand to get things going."

"Wouldn't you want all the money at one time since your wife is sick?" Bryce questioned.

"Don't worry about that part. I wouldn't turn over the deed until it's paid for though. We can go over the details if you're really serious about it."

"Trust me, I'm serious. This could be my comeback." Bryce couldn't wipe the smile off of his face. "I can't wait to tell Seven."

Bryce shook Darrell's hand and hurried out of the office. As he thought about how he could make this happen, his stomach started to growl even louder. Too proud to ask anyone to borrow some money for food, Bryce pulled out his wallet even though he knew it was empty. He'd given Seven his last forty dollars for gas. After staring at a small picture of her that he'd tucked behind his license, he started to shake his head.

"You're right baby. Something needs to happen for us. If not, I might lose you and that can't happen."

BEDROOM GANGSTA

Chapter Four

As Seven prepared the next client to be shampooed, she couldn't help but think about her and Bryce's argument earlier that morning. Throwing the black cape around Hypnotic's body and fastening it tightly around her neck, Seven wondered if Bryce had given any thought to her going back to dance. Even though money was mainly the reason why she wanted to return, Seven had to admit she missed her mini celebrity status. Sure, she got plenty of attention from Bryce along with gawks and stares from dudes on the street, but that didn't compare to the way she was treated at Temptations.

Even if I could go back for at least one night a week, that would help, she thought.

The chair jerked like a roller coaster ride as she leaned Hypnotic back into the shampoo bowl. However, instead of testing the temperature of the water when she turned it on, Seven just picked up the hose and drenched Hypnotic's hair.

Hypnotic immediately sat up. "What are you doing? That shit is too cold!" she yelled.

"Oh, my goodness. I'm so sorry," Seven replied adjusting the handles on the faucet.

Using her hands to test the water this time, when the temperature was just right Seven pulled Hypnotic back down into the bowl. "Sorry, again girl. My mind was somewhere else for a minute."

"It's cool," Hypnotic said, realizing that Seven had never done that before. "Just don't let it happen again, since you work off tips," she responded.

Seven stared at Hypnotic trying to let her know that her joke wasn't the least bit amusing, but by that time Hypnotic had closed her eyes in an attempt to get comfortable.

Trying to brush it off, Seven poured a large amount of pear scented shampoo into her hands, before applying it to Hypnotic's hair. Seconds later she began massaging Hypnotic's scalp in a circular motion sending her into complete relaxation mode.

"Damn Seven, you really know how to work your fingers," Hypnotic said. "I feel like I'm at some upscale spa whenever I'm in here."

"Thanks," Seven responded in a dry tone.

It was hard for her to appreciate the compliment when she hated the job so much. Not to mention, Hypnotic irritated her most of the time. They'd known each other for years since both women were dancers at the strip club. But even back then it seemed as if Hypnotic was always taking cheap shots or had something sarcastic to say. At first she thought Hypnotic was just simply being competitive, but now since Seven was out of the business it was confirmed that Hypnotic was simply a bitch.

"So, how are things going? I haven't been here in a while," Hypnotic said trying to make small talk.

"Things are okay," Seven responded. *If she's trying to get in my business, she can cancel that shit.*

"That's good to hear. I remembered when I first heard that you'd stopped dancing and was working at a salon I thought your ass was crazy, cuz I know the money can't be the same. But as long as you're happy that's all that matters."

Seven refused to feed too much into the conversation. "Yep. I'm happy." She turned the water back on to wash the shampoo out before doing the process all over again.

"Well, business has been crazy for me. There's been all kinds of major parties around town, so I'm killing 'em. My black book stays booked up," Hypnotic boasted out of nowhere.

"Is that right," Seven replied unenthused. *I forgot how her ass never shuts up once she starts talking about herself,* Seven thought. *She's always bragging about shit.*

Washing the shampoo out again, Seven rung a little bit of water out before applying some conditioner. "So, you must be making good money."

"Damn right I am. Shit, I just got a new 2011 Benz."

Feeling a little jealous, Seven used more ice cold water to rinse the conditioner off which caused Hypnotic to jump. "My bad, girl," Seven replied as if it was an accident. "I don't know what's wrong with me and this water today."

"It's cool. I know you didn't do it on purpose," Hypnotic replied. "Anyway, I wish you were still in the business because it's a lot of money coming back to New Orleans. It's so much that I'm thinking about opening up my own escort service. But I wanna do something different with mine though. Instead of women, I just wanna hire men. That's going to be my little niche. A good male escort could break the bank in a time like this," Hypnotic continued. "I need fine men though. I don't want no average dudes."

Seven really wasn't paying Hypnotic any attention until suddenly a picture of Bryce popped into her head. He fit the criteria perfectly. *Oh shit, something like that would work, especially with Bryce. He's extremely attractive and has a body of a twenty year old. All the bitches used to sweat his ass whenever he came to the club, so I know women would love to date him. Plus, when you throw in the fact that he's amazing in bed, it seems as if he was born to do this shit,* she thought. A large smile took over her face as she pictured Bryce coming home with stacks of money. *Hell, by being an escort maybe his ass can get me back to the lifestyle that I'm supposed to be living.*

"Girl, I see you smiling. My idea is the bomb, huh? If I get the right man who can start things off, then eventually help me bring in other guys, this shit could really work. I could be sitting back collecting money like Gwen was doing with us,"

Hypnotic commented.

The mention of Gwen's name instantly made Seven feel uneasy. Although most people knew she was a stripper, there were only a select few who knew she also dabbled in the escort business at one point. After meeting Gwen in Temptations one night, the feisty, petite older woman recruited both Seven and Hypnotic to her company. Seven held down both jobs for about three months, and although the money was excellent she eventually decided that escorting wasn't for her. Seven didn't have a problem with showing off her naked body to strange men, but sleeping with them wasn't something she could get used to. While Seven went back to Temptations full time, Hypnotic stayed with Gwen.

"I couldn't stand Gwen's ass. I mean she was a bitch twenty-four hours a day. Is she still the same?" Seven questioned.

"I don't know. I left her about two months ago."

Seven looked down, staring at Hypnotic's exaggerated eyelashes. "Stop lying, how the hell did that happen?" After sitting Hypnotic up in the chair, Seven wrapped a towel around her head.

"Well, not only was I finally fed up with Gwen's attitude, but I just sat down one day and realized that her ass was making all this money off of me and she wasn't doing shit," Hypnotic answered. "I was the one doing all the fucking while she sat back collecting the money, so I rolled out. Plus, I had a weird feeling that she was stealing money from me."

"How?"

"I don't wanna get into it since I don't have any proof, but either way it's all good because I learned more than enough to start my own shit, which is what I've been doing ever since. Now, I book my own dates, and don't have to share the profits with anyone."

"I can't believe you left. So, what's it like being on your own?" Seven was finally interested in what she had to say.

"You're asking a lot of questions. Are you working for

the cops now?" Hypnotic joked.

"No, I'm just curious, I guess. I was in the game so I know how hard it is being out on your own."

Hypnotic smiled. "Girl please, it hasn't been hard for me. Shit, these muthafuckas out here can't get enough."

With a cocoa colored complexion, and big eyes, Seven didn't think Hypnotic was much of a looker. However, she could never hate on the girl's body. She was stacked with a perfect sized waist, and a huge Nicki Minaj ass.

"I'm doing good for myself, but I still need to find some guys and get my company going," Hypnotic continued.

"You know what, now that I think about it, I'm not sure if it's a lot of women out here willing to pay for an escort. Where would you find clients? How much would you charge? How far would you expect the guys to go?"

"I would want their ass to go all the way. Girl, you would be surprised how many lonely women are out here looking for a man, but can't find one. Just like all the desperate ass men out here, there are plenty of desperate ass women willing to pay for a date or a good fuck. My company would provide sexy, good looking men to women who are either too busy to find a man or not cute enough to get one," Hypnotic said with a huge laugh.

"Wow," Seven replied as she continued to dry Hypnotic's hair. "What about the money?"

"Another question. Girl, it sounds like you're doing an interrogation at the police station. Why…do you know a guy who would be great for the position?"

"No," Seven said after a long pause. "I was just wondering, that's all."

"Well, to answer your question, I guess the eighty/twenty rule works for me. I mean, I'm paying for the operation out of pocket. All the nigga gotta do is show up, have fun, lay some fucking pipe and bring home the money."

"So what's the penalty for breaking the rules?" Seven asked. "What if he tries to book a job on the side?"

"I haven't gotten that far yet. It's a plan in progress. You asking questions like you're interested in coming back to work."

Seven shook her head. "No…that line of work isn't for me anymore. Again, I was just curious since the idea seemed so interesting."

"I was getting ready to say. I knew your husband would-n't go for that shit," Hypnotic replied.

The loud sound of heels clanking against the marble floor made both of them look over. It was Camille, the owner of the salon and Hypnotic's hairstylist walking in their direction.

"Hey Seven, is Hypnotic ready for the dryer?" Camille asked.

Seven looked at her boss whose big eyes and full lips re-minded her of Taraji P. Henson. Not to mention, her bob-styled hair was always full of body.

"I was just about to walk her over," Seven answered.

"I see you let your hair grow out some," Camille said, rubbing her hands through Hypnotic's short locks.

"Yeah, I've been wearing a lot of wigs lately, so that's why I haven't been here that often. See in my line of work, I need to be a different person every night," Hypnotic advised.

Camille laughed showing her expensive veneers. "And on that note, Seven just pre-dry her for about fifteen minutes. I'll blow dry the rest."

Seven nodded. "Okay."

After walking Hypnotic over to the dryers that were lined against the wall, Seven handed her an Essence magazine then turned the dryer on.

"I'll be back to get you in a few minutes," Seven said.

"And I'll be right here," Hypnotic replied. "Try to think of some men for me while I'm under here. Your ass had good clients at the club."

"Will do," Seven said in a fake tone.

Hypnotic had just sat down in Camille's chair when the

door opened and a tall, beautiful woman walked in. Demanding attention, everyone in the shop turned to look at the Chanel purse carrying woman who looked fabulous in her studded Valentino dress. As the woman strutted up to the receptionist desk wearing nude Christian Louboutin Daffodil pumps, Seven remembered the days of wearing $2,500.00 dresses and $1,000.00 shoes.

"Hello, do you have an appointment?" the receptionist asked.

"Angelique, is that you?" Hypnotic shouted from Camille's chair.

"Hey girl, I had the hardest time finding this shop. I feel like a fish out of water trying to get around the city," Angelique said, walking around the desk.

"Camille, I want you to meet my cousin Angelique. She just moved here from Houston and she's looking for a good hairstylist, so of course I told her about you," Hypnotic praised.

"Thanks for the referral. It's nice to meet you cousin," Camille replied.

"I really need my hair done. Can you take me today?" Angelique asked.

Camille stared at Angelique for a few seconds. "That's a weave right?"

Angelique played with her twenty-two inch locks. "Yeah, but don't worry. I just need it washed for now. Nothing major."

"Okay, well if that's all you need then you're in luck because my next appointment cancelled," Camille advised.

Angelique smiled. "That works for me."

"Hey Seven, please take her to the back," Camille instructed.

"Cuz, that's my girl Seven. We used to work at Temptations together. She'll treat you real good unless her mind is on something else," Hypnotic said with a smile.

"Don't show off because your folks are here," Seven said looking over at Hypnotic. "Angelique, you can follow me over to the shampoo area. Don't pay your cousin any attention."

When Seven finished washing Angelique's hair, she was truly impressed with how Seven made her scalp feel and how fast she got her over to the dryers. Because she had a weave, the drying process is what took the longest, but as soon as she was done, Seven walked Angelique back over to Camille's station. The women were laughing and talking loudly about the need of men when Angelique sat down.

"So, what are we discussing ladies?" Angelique asked.

"We were talking about all the possibilities that a good dick could do for a woman with a little money at her disposal," Hypnotic blurted out.

"Oh really, well in that case do you have a number for that good dick because a sister needs to be introduced and taken care of," Angelique chimed back in.

Hypnotic looked directly at Seven. "See, my point has already been proven. A man with a good dick could be King of New Orleans."

"So Camille…Angelique, could either of you see yourselves paying for a male escort?" Seven curiously asked.

"Hell no!" one of the stylists yelled out.

"I wasn't talking to your nosey ass Cee Cee," Seven said shaking her head. "Plus you're knocked up so of course you would say that."

"Well, I'm new in town, and haven't been satisfied in a while, so a man like that would be a dream right about now. He could escort me to different events, show me around, and then bang my brains out. Hell, sign me up right now," Angelique added.

"I know plenty of women, myself included that can't find a good fuck anywhere. If there was a number I could call and get me a guy for a date or weekend getaway with no strings attached, I'd use it," Camille said, handing Hypnotic a small mirror so she could examine her spiky haircut. "I mean if this dude could even come with a money back guarantee if I'm not satisfied, it's a win-win situation for everyone involved. Shit, do you two have a card or number for a man like that?" Camille questioned before pulling off Hypnotic's cape.

"Not yet, but I'm working on it," Hypnotic said standing up. She tapped Seven on the back and winked at her as she walked over to the full length mirror.

"What do you do for a living if you don't mind me asking?" Camille asked Angelique.

"I'm a sports attorney for several big name professional players in the NBA. I even represent a couple baseball players and now a few players on the New Orleans Saints," Angelique answered.

Camille smiled. "You must be rolling in the dough?"

"Angelique is paid with that real money, but I'm gonna catch up to her with my idea. This shit is a guaranteed money maker," Hypnotic butted in then played with a few strands of her hair. "Camille, you did your thing as usual. I'm ready to break some nigga's wallets now."

Camille smiled again.

Hypnotic turned back to Seven. "Okay, so when I get this escort thing off the ground, you come looking for me if you want to get back into the business."

Bitch, you must be simple to think I'd come work for your dumb ass, Seven thought before giving off a phony smile. "Okay."

At that moment, Hypnotic's Blackberry went off. After looking at the number and realizing it was from one of her regulars, she quickly read the text. "Umm Cuz, we're gonna have to take a rain check on those dinner plans we had. Just got a call, so I need to go make some money," Hypnotic said.

"It's cool," Angelique answered.

After giving a few fake air kisses, Hypnotic said goodbye to everyone then made her way to her car that was parked right out front. Desperately wanting to know what she was driving, Seven walked toward the front window and watched as Hypnotic hopped into her cherry red, metallic Mercedes S65 AMG.

This is some bullshit, Seven thought.

Seeing Hypnotic on top of her game, Seven immediately reminisced about all the fancy restaurants she used to go to while escorting, along with the sky box seats to major sporting events, the lavish out of town trips, and most of all the stacks of money she kept in shoe boxes inside her closet. Seven couldn't believe how her life was going and seeing an unworthy bitch like Hypnotic doing so well seemed to co-sign how she was feeling.

"Fuck this," Seven said in a low tone.

At that moment, she stormed to the back of the shop to retrieve her phone from her purse. *I know just who to call to hit me off. I mean Bryce will never have to know where the money came from,* Seven tried to convince herself.

Seven typed in her four letter password to unlock her phone. After clicking on her contacts icon, she had quick little flashbacks with each name she passed with her finger. *I wonder what Bryce thought when he asked me for my password and I refused to give it to him. He would definitely go off if he knew I still had these numbers in my phone,* Seven thought as the list of names from her wild days at Temptations scrolled by. However, she also wasn't stupid. Every name was listed as women, not men.

Seven only kept these numbers in case of a rainy day and it was only getting cloudy. After finding the name she was look-ing for, she hit the call button then waited for him to answer.

Chapter Five

Seven couldn't get the idea of running an escort agency out of her head. She spent the rest of her shift fantasizing about putting Bryce to work, and not having to deal with annoying ass bill collectors anymore. She dreamt about having all her favorite designers like Marc Jacobs, Badgley Mishka and Alexander McQueen back in her closet, and Hypnotic's idea was how she was going to achieve that goal.

Seven rushed home without going for her usual drink at The Cat's Meow with the other girls in the shop. Instead, she wanted to beat Bryce home and do something special for her man. When Seven finally got home, she didn't waste any time jumping into action. After searching the refrigerator for something to throw together, she pulled out a pack of ground beef when she found a box of Hamburger Helper in the back of the pantry. Seven wasn't known for her cooking skills, and could only make simple things like tuna fish, oodles of noodles, and BLT's. Before she started cooking, Seven decided to clean up the small apartment that always seemed to be out of order.

Usually, Seven would bitch and complain when it came to doing any domestic work or she would just leave it for Bryce to organize, but today was different. She needed him to relax when he got home. When Seven finished fluffing the cushions on their old couch and vacuuming the carpet, she made a mental note of everything that was going in the trash as soon as they started making money.

By the time Mitch and Bryce pulled up forty-five minutes later, the street lights were glowing except the one closest to his building. The apartment appeared dark from the curb as Bryce prepared to get out of the car. Bryce glanced over to see the orange light on the dash acknowledging Mitch was low on gas.

"Hey, once I get my check, I'll hook you up with some gas for looking out for me," Bryce said holding out his right fist.

Mitch reached over and gave Bryce a pound. "Nigga, we go back since free lunch. I know you're good for it. If shit was reversed, I know you'd have my back."

"No doubt. Can you come scoop me tomorrow?"

"Of course. Same time," Mitch said just before pulling off.

The sounds of R. Kelly's old hit, *Bump and Grind* could be heard from the second floor as Bryce ascended the staircase. A funny feeling over came him when he realized that the music was coming from his apartment. Normally, Seven didn't listen to music that loud unless she was in a good mood, and since they hadn't spoken to each other all day he had no idea what was going on.

Maybe she got a raise at work or something, Bryce thought as he stuck his key in the door and slowly twisted the knob.

He walked inside the apartment to find Seven sitting on the couch with the red bustier and garter belt set that he'd given her on their first Valentine's Day together.

"Damn, did I come to the right house?" Bryce asked closing the door.

"Yes, you did," Seven replied with a smile. "Baby, I just wanted to apologize for this morning. All day long I've been feeling bad about my behavior. I love you so much."

When Bryce realized that the outfit Seven was wearing was the exact ensemble she wore when she told him she was with child two years ago, he felt butterflies in his stomach. However, the sadness of her telling him that she'd lost the baby a couple of months later invaded his mind at the same time. Bryce quickly remembered the conversation they had when Seven told him that she would go all out if she ever got pregnant again. His heart rate began to increase as he wondered if she was with child.

"So, what's going on?" Bryce eagerly questioned.

Seven walked over and began rubbing Bryce's chest, then gave him a long passionate kiss. "I just felt like doing something nice for the greatest man in the world."

"Okay, now I know I must be in the wrong place now. Either that or I need a hit of whatever you've been smoking."

"Ha, ha. I see you're full of jokes. Listen, sweetheart I wanna share something with you, but first I need for you to go into the bathroom, take your clothes off, then go relax in the hot water waiting for you in the tub. You can eat once you get out," she said, smacking him on the butt.

Damn, whatever she's holding onto must really be something major. I can get used to this, he thought then turned around to walk toward the bathroom.

After quickly taking off his clothes and hopping into the tub, Bryce immediately laid his head back against the white tiled wall. Thinking about Seven's good news, Bryce was so at peace that he didn't even notice when his wife walked into the bathroom a few minutes later and sat down on the toilet. Seven stared at Bryce's huge penis that was lying on his stomach.

She smiled. "There's no shrinking that python."

Before Bryce could respond, Seven slowly slithered off the toilet and kneeled down next to the tub. Her cold hand startled Bryce as she slid it down toward his unsuspecting shaft.

"Oh shit," Bryce said splashing water on Seven's sexy outfit.

"I love seeing my man in his birthday suit."

"Well, I hope you like what you see."

"Maybe," Seven said with a little laugh.

"Maybe? Did I just hear you say maybe?" Bryce asked. Seconds later he snatched Seven by her waist and pulled her into the tub.

"Bryce you better not get my hair wet!" she shouted.

"I remember when we used to sweat your hairstyle out every night when we first met and you never complained."

"Well that was when we had money to get it done. Camille doesn't do my hair for free you know. She's all about her paper." Seven quickly paused once she saw Bryce's face start to tense up.

"Go ahead and finish what you were about to say," he encouraged.

Seven ignored his request and planted a long kiss on Bryce's lips. She then grabbed his growing dick and massaged it until it was at full attention. Seven began to maneuver her body to a more comfortable position when suddenly the smoke alarm alerted that their dinner might be burning.

"Oh shit. I forgot that I was warming the food. Push me up!" Seven yelled.

The smoke had quickly filled a small portion of the apartment by the time Seven ran into the kitchen. She quickly turned the burner off and slid the pan to the middle of the stove. Seconds later, Bryce walked in with a towel around his waist to see Seven waving a broom back and forth. She was desperately trying to clear the area around the detector to stop it from blasting. Bryce pulled off his towel and began helping her fan the room. As his dick swung side to side, it immediately caught Seven's eye. With his body hard to resist, her juices started to matriculate between her legs instantly.

It made her smile knowing that he belonged to her. Forgetting all about the detector, she dropped to her knees and wrapped her lips around his dick. Like the amateur porn star she was, Seven started sucking, rubbing his balls with one hand and squeezing his naked ass with the other.

Her mouth felt so good, but with the detector still blaring, Bryce needed to make it stop before a neighbor came over or called 911. Picking up the broom Seven had dropped on the floor, Bryce took the handle and knocked the device off the ceiling. As soon as the noise ceased, he reached both of his hands back to hold onto the kitchen counter for support when his legs started to tremble. Moments later, Bryce unloaded a large quantity of semen into her working mouth.

Seven began to choke as some of Bryce's thick cum went down her wind pipe. Even though Bryce felt dizzy, he managed to stoop down and softly pat Seven on her back.

"I thought you were past the choking stage," he joked.

"Shut up. You caught me off guard. Next time, I'll just spit that shit back up instead of trying to swallow when I'm not ready," Seven replied letting out a deep breath.

Bryce continued to rub his wife's back. "You okay?" When Seven nodded her head, they both stood back up. "Thanks for the treat. I was stressed all day until now."

"You're welcome."

"So, what are we going to eat now? I didn't eat lunch so I'm starving," Bryce said looking over at the burnt pan of food. "I'm glad I didn't marry you for your cooking."

"Real funny," Seven responded. "It's not much in here. How about a peanut butter and honey sandwich?"

"Honey? Don't you mean jelly."

"Well we're out of jelly, so honey is the closest thing we have."

"That'll work. I'm so hungry I'll eat almost anything," Bryce replied.

"I'll remind you of that last statement when we're in bed tonight," she said, winking her eye.

Once they got all the ingredients to start making the sandwich, Bryce caught Seven smiling and laughing. "Are you finally gonna share what you're so happy about?" he asked.

"I was just thinking back to a conversation that I had earlier with an old co-worker from back in the day," Seven answered.

"It must've been a good one judging by the size of the

grin on your face."

Seven smiled again then used the butter knife to spread peanut butter on one of the slices of bread. "So, what's going on with the money and the bills? Will the rent be paid or are we gonna be homeless?"

Bryce let out a long sigh. "Baby, don't worry yourself with the rent money. I'm working on it. I still have some other possibilities that might pan out. I'll make a way. You'll never have to worry about being homeless."

"So, should I ask my brother for some money?"

Bryce gave Seven a funny look. "Hell no. Every time we get in a bind you always bring him up. I don't always want him in our business. We've borrowed enough from him anyway."

"Stop being so proud, Bryce. If we need the money all I have to do is ask him for it."

"I'm not being proud. I just don't wanna ask the nigga for anymore money. I told you I would take care of it."

Since Seven's drug dealer brother, Stephon was the only family she had, normally Bryce didn't say anything when she brought his name up. But borrowing money from him consistently really did make Bryce feel less than a man. He'd never met her crackhead mother, who Seven never spoke about, and her father was nonexistent.

"Why don't you let me go back to the club and strip for a minute or two? That'll get us out of the red in no time."

"Look, I already told you that no wife of mine is going to be showing off her naked body to a bunch of horny fucking men. Disrespectful men who think strippers are a bunch of hoes."

"Is that what you thought when you were waving your hundred dollar bills and stuffing them into my g-string? It was okay that I was a stripper when you wanted me, but now it's out of the question since you got me," Seven said, slamming the knife on the counter.

"Don't try and put extra words in my mouth. All I'm saying is that part of your life is over so there's no need for you to go back in the past. I'll find a way and make this thing work for us," Bryce replied.

A devilish smirk took over her face. "Well, since you don't want me to go back and strip and *you* want to be the one to bring us out of this, I have another idea that would bring us some money."

"Oh yeah, I can't wait to hear what that idea might be," Bryce said, closing the lid on the Jif jar.

"How do you feel about escort services?"

Bryce immediately started laughing. "Escort Services? If I don't want you to go back to the strip club, then why would I agree to you becoming an escort like that's a better job."

Seven's loud burst of laughter made Bryce's laughter seem childlike. "I was referring to you becoming an escort, not me."

Bryce stood frozen. "What did you just say?"

"I said, I was talking about you becoming an escort, not me. I know a lot of women who would pay big money for a date with a good looking man like yourself," Seven informed.

"Now, I know you've been sniffing too many of those fucking chemicals at the salon to say some dumb shit like that. You've really lost your mind," Bryce responded. "I hope that wasn't what you were excited to share with me." He was beginning to realize that Seven probably wasn't pregnant.

"You know what…I must've lost my mind giving up my life to follow a man who can't even pay the fucking bills," Seven shot back. She wiped her hand across the counter sending all the food and dishes to the floor. "I don't deserve this shit. Look at what we're eating. I don't wanna struggle. I deserve three course meals!"

Bryce couldn't believe her outburst. "So, you'd rather throw our wedding vows out the window just because we hit a bad patch? You mean to tell me that you wouldn't mind me being with other women? Trust me the first time we have a fight, you'll use that shit against me faster than the Indy 500."

"You've been with another woman before, remember?"

Bryce paused for a moment. "What?"

"You heard me. Don't get amnesia on me now. You don't remember when all you talked about was seeing me with another woman on your birthday that year. I went out and found you one who didn't have a problem with you watching. Then in the middle, I got bored with her and asked you to come over and join us. You didn't have a problem with fucking another woman then, so why now."

"I didn't want to fuck her. I just wanted to watch two women go at it," Bryce replied.

"It didn't seem like you had a problem sticking your dick in her to me!"

"That was years ago when we were dating. I haven't asked for anything like that since. Plus you want me to fuck a lot of women not just one."

"Okay, I get it now. When I asked you to join us that wasn't bad. But since I want you to get paid for the sex now, that idea sounds crazy. So, you'll fuck a woman for free, but a bitch paying you is out of the question. Yeah, that makes a lot of sense," Seven said, then stormed out the kitchen.

"You can try and twist this shit all you want. I'll fix cars in the damn street before I prostitute myself for a buck!" Bryce yelled back. "And you better not think I'm cleaning this shit up!"

Bryce could hear Seven's footsteps stop then come back toward him. "Hey, I think Jiffy Lube is hiring if all you wanna do is be a fucking grease monkey. I hate niggas with no ambition."

Bryce didn't respond. Instead, he walked toward her. Seven assumed he was about to go off, but he kept going past her. Bryce returned moments later with a pair of running shorts and a white t-shirt. He went over and grabbed the car key off the glass table.

"Where the fuck do you think you're going with my car?" Seven barked.

"Out."

Bryce snatched the door open and slammed it behind him. Seconds later he could hear the door opening. Seven ran over to the rail and leaned over. "If you're taking my car, that's all the gas I have to get me back and forth to work. You better not use it up!"

Bryce didn't even look back. After getting in the car, he quickly put Seven's Hyundai Sonata in drive and sped off down the street. Going well beyond the speed limit, Bryce drove to a twenty-four hour liquor store cursing the entire time. He pulled into the parking lot and lifted up the back seat floor mat and retrieved a twenty dollar bill that he hid for emergencies. Going into the store, he came back out moments later with a small bottle of Ciroc.

Bryce had nowhere to go, but he knew he wasn't going back home to a disrespectful wife at the moment. Instead, he began driving all around town drinking straight from the bottle. "I can't believe she wants me to fuck other women for money. She can't love me saying shit like that," he said to himself.

Bryce had only been driving a short time, but the bottle was half-way gone by the time he turned onto English Turn Drive, an upscale section of New Orleans where the homes started at $500,000 and neighbored the prestigious English Turn Golf & County Club. It was also a section of the city where all the street lights worked, there was no trash blowing all around, and best of all, there were no thugs hanging out on every corner.

Pulling the car over, Bryce leaned back in his seat and turned the bottle upside down until his throat burned from the warm liquid. Looking at one of the huge mansions, Bryce envisioned himself pulling up from work to find Seven and two small children running up to his car with huge smiles. Bryce took another drink as he then imagined his yard filled with family and friends at their annual Fourth of July cook-out. He desperately wanted to move Seven from their tiny apartment to a nice size home down in Houston. He wanted to get out of New Orleans, especially after hearing about so many people making it big in Texas. Bryce continued to take the vodka to the head until it was only a little left. At that moment, he started to contemplate if Seven's idea was truly that bad. However, that thought only took a few seconds to disregard before he took another swig to finish off the bottle and said, "Hell no. I'm not doing that shit."

Chapter Six

The next day, Bryce searched through all the drawers looking for his wrench to remove a bolt on the timing belt job he was working on. He opened and slammed each metal box with severe force. His loud and constant outbursts of "shit and damn" made the customers sitting in the waiting area wonder what was going on.

"Who moved my fucking wrench?" Bryce yelled.

The other mechanics didn't respond. They knew something major was bothering Bryce and if he didn't want to discuss it, none of them were about to play Dr. Phil. They all kept working with their heads down pretending to be oblivious to his rants and raves.

With the due date for the rent money closing in on him, and Seven giving him the silent treatment for the past two days, Bryce was in a terrible mood. Normally at desperate times like this he could go to Mitch for help since he had two jobs. As Lead Forman of Douglas Construction and the bartender gig at Temptations, Mitch would often loan Bryce money. But this time Mitch's cash was tied up from all the renovations he'd done to his house, along with his mother's. Bryce's options seemed to be exhausted.

When Bryce found the wrench he was looking for, it was next to another mechanic's work station. "Reggie, don't touch

my shit if you're not gonna put it back where you found it,"
Bryce snapped.

"Nigga, you need to switch to decaf. Damn, I was just
borrowing it," Reggie shot back.

"Look, just leave my shit alone!" Bryce shouted.

"What's going on in here?" Darrell said, walking into the
garage.

"I was looking for my wrench and couldn't find it because niggas don't know how to put my shit back," Bryce responded.

"Are you crazy? I can hear you all the way in my office,
and I'm sure the customers waiting can, too," Darrell stated.

"Sorry D. I just got a lot on my mind," Bryce said, rubbing his head.

"That's understandable, but you gotta maintain your
composure. Why don't you come and talk with me in my office
to clear your head? I need to talk with you about something anyway," Darrell said, patting Bryce on the back.

Assuming this private meeting was for Darrell to give
him the money he needed to pay his rent, Bryce's attitude
quickly changed. He threw the wrench onto the metal cabinet,
then followed Darrell in the back. Before Darrell could say a
word, Bryce was already thanking him.

"What are you thanking me for? You haven't even heard
what I have to say yet," Darrell said, sitting down behind his
oak desk.

Bryce pulled out the other chair and sat down. "Okay
then, what's up?"

"First, how's Symone?" Darrell asked calling Seven by
her real name. "I haven't seen her around in a while."

"She's fine."

"That's's good. Anyway, I want to tell you that even
though you haven't been here as long as the other guys, I think
of you like a son. It was my dream in life to leave this place to a
family member, but I've out lived anyone worth taking the
reigns," Darrell advised.

"What are you trying to get at?" Bryce asked realizing that Darrell wasn't heading in the direction of giving him any money.

"My wife's health has taken a turn for the worse, so I might have to leave sooner than expected. I didn't want you to forget about taking over the garage. I want you to work hard at trying to come up with the money because I really don't wanna sell it to someone else," Darrell responded.

Bryce dropped his head into his chest. He was happy that Darrell wanted to leave the garage to him, but his concern about being evicted was much more important.

"I'm thinking you only got about three months to come up with the money now," Darrell added.

Instead of replying, Bryce got up and walked back into the garage. He wasn't in the mood to talk about owning the garage, especially since his rent was top priority at the moment. He needed a solution, and he needed it quick.

Bryce was having trouble putting a new battery inside a car when the ground shaking bass from a snow white Range Rover turning into the parking lot caught his attention. Wondering who it was, Bryce let out a long sigh when Seven's brother Stephon stepped out a few minutes later.

I wonder what he wants, Bryce thought. *I'ma kill Seven if she called him anyway.*

"What up Bryce?" Stephon shouted as he walked toward the bay doors.

Stephon stood six feet with long shoulder length dreads and an iced out platinum grill that matched the crucifix around his neck. A walking billboard for Gucci and Louis Vuitton, Bryce absolutely hated his brother-in-law's flashy ways.

"What do you want?" Bryce replied in a low tone.

"Damn, is that the way you greet fam, nigga?" Stephon's powerful laugh went with his commanding two hundred pound stature. "I need a little help. I need some chrome rims to trick out my new ride. I was hopin' to throw some money your way if you do the job."

Bryce held up a socket wrench. "Are you trying to be funny? Stephon, you know my shop went belly-up. I don't do that shit any more. Come back when you need a tune-up or something."

"Yeah, that's right. I forgot."

That nigga ain't forget shit. I hate his fake ass. He always trying to flex like he's this drug lord and making money hands over fist. If he wasn't Seven's folks, I would knock his punk ass out, Bryce thought.

"Well, even though you don't have your shop anymore, I know you still got the hook up on rims and shit. I got my eye on these Dub's," Stephon added.

"Whatever contacts I had are long gone, so I can't help you," Bryce replied nonchalantly. "Besides, you got money so why do you need a hook up?"

Stephon walked over and stood in front of Bryce. "Nigga, what's your problem? I got plenty of money, but what the fuck does that have to do with anything. After all the help I give to you and Seven, you can't hook a brother up. Whenever she calls for a loan, it's me tossin' out rolls to keep y'all lights on and shit. You need to show me a little more respect."

Bryce stepped back. "I've never asked your sister to call and get a loan from you. I can handle my household."

"I never saw Seven bring any of the money back because her man was takin' care of business either. Besides, I give the money to Seven to take care of her needs. If she uses it to take care of yours then you should be thankin' me," Stephon said getting loud.

Bryce looked around the garage. With everyone staring down their throats by now, he was completely embarrassed. "Nigga, you must be high. Did you say I should be thanking you? That shit will never happen!" Bryce shouted.

Stephon started to shake his head. "That shit must really

burn you up when you have to use my money to take care of your house."

Bryce bit the inside of his cheek to keep from punching Stephon in his face. "Next time your sister calls and asks for a little help, you tell her that I said fuck you and your money."

Stephon laughed. "You sound like a fool. I'll never let my sister go without," he said walking back toward his truck.

"We don't need your fucking money! I can provide for my wife!" Bryce shouted as the other mechanics looked on.

"You go ahead and take care of your wife. No matter what you say, if my sister needs me, I'm gonna do whatever I can. Seven will never have to struggle as long as I'm around!" Stephon shouted as he opened his door and got in.

"You keep poking your nose in my business and I'll make sure you're not around anymore!" Bryce yelled as Stephon started his truck and blasted *9 Piece* by Rick Ross.

"I'ma ignore that threat muthafucka," Stephon responded. "But hey, do me a favor. When you get home, tell Seven I always got her back. Even when your broke ass don't," Stephon said before turning up the volume and speeding out of the lot.

By the time Stephon made it to the corner, you could almost see steam coming out of Bryce's ears. Furious, he threw the wrench across the ground, then stormed out of the shop. *I need to get this fucking money fast.*

Bryce walked around for hours before deciding to catch the RTA bus home instead of calling Mitch to come pick him up. He thought real hard as the bus made several stops before letting him off around the corner from his house. Bryce only nodded his head as Moochie tried to start up a conversation when he approached his door.

"Fuck you then," Bryce heard Moochie say when she realized he was ignoring her.

After walking into a completely dark apartment, Bryce noticed that it was almost eight o'clock, so he didn't call out for Seven. He just assumed that she was exhausted from her day at the salon and had fallen asleep in the bedroom. Hoping she'd at least cooked, Bryce looked around the kitchen for a plate, but didn't find one on the counter, the stove or the microwave. He even opened the refrigerator, but didn't find one there either.

"Shit," he said, slamming the refrigerator door.

He could care less if the noise woke Seven up since she hadn't bothered to feed him after a long, stressful day. With an instant attitude, Bryce walked into the bedroom and clicked on the light. It surprised him to find the covers still crumbled up at the foot of the bed from earlier that morning and Seven no where to be found.

Bryce went back to the kitchen and grabbed the last two beers out of the refrigerator. He then walked over, plopped on the couch and flipped through the channels on the television. Bryce stopped on ESPN to catch up on the last bit of highlights on SportsCenter. Minutes later, he pulled out his cell phone and dialed Seven's number. After a couple of rings it went to her voicemail.

Maybe she went out with some of the girls from work, Bryce thought as he tossed the first beer back.

By the time SportsCenter went off a few minutes later, Seven still hadn't returned his call. He called her a couple more times, but kept getting her voicemail. When an hour passed and she still hadn't responded, Bryce instantly began to worry about his wife's whereabouts. Right when he was about to call once again, his cell phone finally rang.

"Where the hell are you?" Bryce shouted into the phone. He hadn't even bothered to look at the caller id.

"Maybe I should be asking you that. Why didn't your punk ass call to tell me that you had a way home?" Mitch inquired.

"Oh shit. I thought you were Seven," Bryce replied.

"When I went to pick you up Reggie told me that you

walked out today. He said that you seemed pretty upset when you left, and didn't tell anyone where you were going."

"Man, I had so much going on in my head that it totally slipped my mind to call and tell you that I'd rolled out. My bad," Bryce said.

"It's cool. So, are you alright?" Mitch asked.

"Not really. I gotta lot of issues going on right now with these bills and shit. On top of that now my boss wants to sell the garage. He wants me to make an offer on the place."

"I see why you're stressed, but that sounds like a good stress to me. How long did he give you to come up with the cash?" Mitch inquired.

"Just a few months so I gotta get some more money flowing into this house."

"Well, you should be okay since Seven is back working, right?" Mitch asked puzzling Bryce. "Why didn't you tell me that she was coming back to work?"

"What the hell are you talking about?" Bryce asked as his face began to turn to stone.

"When I walked in the club a few minutes ago I saw Seven going into the dancer's locker room. At first, I thought she was just here to visit, but the owner told me that tonight would be a good one since his star, Seven was back. You didn't know she was working again."

Bryce couldn't believe his ears. *How the fuck could she go behind my back to that damn spot after I told her that shit wasn't a fucking option.* He became enraged with the thoughts of men staring and touching Seven as she did her performance.

"Hey, I need you to come pick me up right now," Bryce said.

"Damn, by the sound of your voice I guess you didn't know," Mitch responded. "I wish I could man, but I just got to the club and my shift is about to start. We're short handed tonight so I can't roll out."

Bryce pulled out his wallet. He searched through all the pockets until he found a folded ten dollar bill. He then went through all his pants pockets until he pulled out three crumbled up one dollar bills. Thirteen dollars was all he had to hopefully get him down there.

"Look, I'm on my way down there. Don't let Seven leave until I get there!" Bryce said before hanging up.

Chapter Seven

When the cab door opened, Bryce stepped out still wearing his navy blue, oil stained work jumpsuit. He could still hear the driver cursing him out since he was two dollars short of the fare. The driver even threatened to call the police, but Bryce knew the local 5-0 had better shit to do than settling a two dollar dispute. As soon as he walked up to the front door, Bryce already had his ID out to make the process faster.

"It's a ten dollar cover and a two drink minimum," the bouncer said once he handed Bryce his license back.

"I'm not staying. I just came to get my wife then we're leaving," Bryce replied.

"Your wife? I don't think you have the right place. I hope you're not talking about one of the strippers because I know ain't none of them married," the bouncer responded.

Bryce tried to walk around the huge Fat Joe looking guy. "I know my wife is in there. Mitch just told me she was."

He looked Bryce up and down. "Mitch called you…yeah right. Look main man, I just started working here so I'm not used to all the fake lines, but I know that's bullshit. It's ten dollars or you can wait out here for whoever to come out," he said blocking Bryce's path.

"Man, get the fuck out of my way! I need to go get my wife!" Bryce shouted.

"Didn't I tell you to back up?"

All the yelling suddenly made the owner, Speedy walk out to investigate. "What's the problem Big Henry?"

"This guy says that his wife is inside and he's here to get her," Big Henry answered.

"Speedy, I'm Seven's husband. Mitch told me that she was down here. I think she's gonna dance, so I'm here to stop her before she makes a huge mistake," Bryce informed.

"Oh yeah, I remember you," Speedy said. "Look, I understand how you feel, but your wife is an adult and can make up her own mind if she wants to work or not. Why don't you come in, have a drink on the house and the two of you can talk it out after she's done."

Bryce wanted to reply to his 'after she's done' comment, but realized he was wasting time. "I'm not gonna make a scene. I just want to talk to her," he advised.

"It's okay Big Henry. I'll take him in and see if I can find Seven so this won't get ugly," Speedy said waving for Bryce to follow him inside.

"What's up Bryce? I see you made it," Mitch said when Speedy and Bryce got over to the bar.

"Hey, give him whatever he wants on the house," Speedy directed to Mitch. "I'll go see if I can find Seven."

"Nigga, I thought you were joking about being on your way down here," Mitch said once Speedy walked off.

"Why? This shit ain't a game. I'ma drag her ass out of here if she gets up on that fucking stage," Bryce answered.

Before Mitch could respond the colored disco ball on the ceiling lit up and began turning around. Knowing exactly what that meant, Bryce turned to face the black curtains on the stage. He ignored Mitch tapping his shoulder when his Long Island Iced Tea was ready and focused his attention on the DJ positioned a few feet away from the stage.

"Good evening to all you big ballers, players and playettes. Man, do I have a special treat for all of you tonight. Coming to the stage is a woman who really needs no introduction. All of the regulars voted her *Most Flexible* eight consecutive times and she's back after a long extended vacation. Let's get those umbrella's ready cause it's time to make it rain. I present the one, the only…"

When the DJ blasted, *Lick* by Jodeci, all the regulars immediately knew who was coming out on stage. The guys started yelling and reaching into their pockets for extra money immediately.

"Put your hands together and give a warm welcome home for everyone's favorite… Seven!" the DJ shouted.

As Bryce's temples began to throb, Seven stepped out from between the curtains wearing a pair of clear five inch platform heels and a hot pink, sequined thong. Following tradition, she wore a set of strawberry nipple covers with her hair settled into a high pony tail.

Bryce turned around and tossed back his drink as his emotions began to increase. He couldn't believe his wife had gone behind his back after he banned her from dancing again. He shook his head as Seven switched her hips and slowly walked toward the gold pole in the center of the stage. She stepped one foot in front of the other like a tight rope performer at the circus. The men instantly started throwing money. As Seven danced very elegantly, her body seemed to hypnotize the onlookers with each twirl or fashion model pose.

"Hey, be cool, man," Mitch said when Bryce started banging his fist against the bar.

"Naw, fuck that," Bryce said standing up.

Seven slid her hand up and down the pole as she prepared to dazzle the crowd with a quadruple spin. She hit a flash dance move and was just about to hit another one when Seven suddenly noticed Bryce coming toward her. She instantly froze.

Just as Bryce was about to leap onto the end of the stage, several bouncers charged at him, instantly pulling his body toward the floor.

"Take his dumb ass out so we can see the show!" a man yelled from a private table.

"But she's my wife!" Bryce belted just as the bouncers picked him up and ushered him toward the front door.

Seven desperately wanted to continue her set, but after seeing the disgusted look on her husband's face, she quickly took off her heels and bolted off the stage.

"I don't want to talk about it anymore!" Seven yelled then walked into the apartment.

Slamming the front door, Bryce quickly followed behind his wife wanting more answers. They'd been arguing all the way home. "I don't understand how you could do that shit to me! Do you know how embarrassing that was to get kicked out the club? I thought I'd made myself clear when I told you that dancing was off limits!"

"You're not my father. I'ma grown ass woman who can make decisions for myself, especially when it's about my life," Seven replied.

"Are you serious? I feel so fucking betrayed right now and you wanna act like you didn't do shit."

"What did I do but try and help us out?"

"Let me run it down for you again since you obviously have fucking amnesia. First, we had an agreement about you going back to work. Second, I called you several times and you didn't answer. That's the same as lying since your ass was at the club and didn't want me to know."

"There goes that daddy attitude again. For your information I didn't answer because I was busy talking to people and didn't hear my phone ringing. Second, what the fuck is the big deal? I went to make us some money. You act as if I destroyed the world. I did what I needed to do for *us*, and that's the only thing you should focus on."

"You've lost complete sense of reality. I told you that I was gonna handle this and that we were gonna be okay. I need you to trust me and have faith that all of this will work itself out!" Bryce shouted.

"Look, I just don't think you know how you're gonna get the money, and instead of being a man about it by telling the truth, you wanna play games."

"I got this!" Bryce shouted even louder. Her true feelings stung.

"You keep saying that, but you never seem to add the part that explains how you're actually going to do it!" Seven yelled back.

At that moment, Mookie started banging on the wall as a signal that she was tired of all the ranting.

"Whatever it is, it won't consist of you swinging your ass in front of a bunch of niggas, that's for damn sure."

"Didn't you see those dumb motherfucka's throwing all that money on the stage when I walked out? We could've paid some of the overdue bills and then some," Seven responded.

Bryce sighed. "For the last time, I don't want my wife stripping. I'll find a way to pay all our bills and get us moving in the right direction."

Seven walked over to the kitchen counter. She pulled out an envelope from a little wicker basket next to the microwave and tossed it toward Bryce. "What are you gonna do about this shit?"

"What's this?" Bryce replied bending over to pick up the envelope.

"It's the fucking cell phone bill!" Seven ranted.

There was a big red Final Notice on the top of the first page. When Bryce looked at the $376.45 due amount, he got an instant headache.

"When it rains it pours," Bryce whispered to his self.

"Well, it ain't just raining, it's the second Katrina. You told me you were going to fix this without my help, but shit seems to be getting worse."

When Bryce stared at his wife, he saw the disgust in her eyes. Reflecting back to the conversation in Darrell's office, now his back was really against the wall.

"Listen, I'm way over my head right now, and I don't know how to get us out of this situation," he finally confessed. "Darrell is gonna put the garage up for sale because his wife is sick and he wants me to buy it. Everything is just coming at me so fast. I do need your help, but there's no way in the world you're going back to that fucking strip club," Bryce said grabbing both of Seven's hands.

"If you don't want me to dance, I don't see any other way out of this not unless you agree to that escorting thing we talked about the other day." Bryce looked like he wanted to say something, but Seven quickly cut him off. "Look, we need fast money right now. Not some part time, minimum wage bullshit."

Bryce rubbed his temples in a circular motion. It felt like his back was against the wall. It took several minutes for him to respond. "I need for you to promise me that if I do this, you won't ever let it come between us. I don't want to lose you trying to make money. I have to know that at the end of this endeavor, you'll still be right by my side."

"Baby!" Seven shouted jumping into Bryce's arms. "I love you. I knew you weren't gonna let me down. Nothing is ever gonna come between that. We're made for each other. I'm not going anywhere, I promise."

"Wow! I haven't seen you this excited in a long time. I hope you know that I'm only going to do this until we're caught up and have a little nest egg," Bryce advised.

"I know," Seven replied with a smile. "And I have the perfect person to be our very first client."

Already...damn I wonder how long she's been planning this shit, Bryce thought. "And who might that be?"

"Ms. Medley," Seven said in a low tone.

A naked vision of Ms. Medley's body immediately rushed into Bryce's head. As a frown formed on his face, he tried to shake the thought of her huge breast hanging down to the floor and the stretch marks that went on for miles.

"You must be crazy. That shit will never happen," Bryce said.

"Why not…she's perfect. It'll knock out the rent money."

"Ms. Medley probably wants her money. She won't agree to what you're thinking. Besides, I'm not gonna trade myself with a woman who lives right downstairs. I'll feel funny every time I see her. Plus, she may want more than I'm willing to give. You ever think about that?" Bryce questioned.

"Well, it's already in place. I was talking with her when I got home from the shop yesterday and she asked me about the rent money. I told her that you were working on it. She made a little slick comment about seeing you naked and hearing us go at it in the mornings. That's when I made reference to you doing some escort type work and she damn near lost her mind."

Bryce was starting to get pissed all over again. "Why were you out promoting something I told you I wasn't going to do?"

"It's just like I told you a second ago. I know my man. We're in this together. You asked me to marry you because you knew I would say yes. I knew you were gonna do whatever it took to provide for me, too."

Bryce sighed and paused for a few seconds. "So, when and where am I supposed to do this shit?"

Seven laughed. "Don't worry. All you have to do is sit and talk with her. She's not looking for sex. She's just a lonely woman who needs a little male companionship," Seven said holding a straight face even though she knew every word was a lie. "I'm not asking for you to cure Cancer, I just found a way for us to make a bunch of money with very little work involved. If you can show her a really good time, she'll forget about the back rent and give us a credit for next month. That means we can use your paycheck to pay the cell phone bill and we're on our way to fixing this shit."

"What if I decide not to do it?" Bryce asked.

Seven frowned. "Then get your cardboard ready because we're gonna be living on the fucking streets.

Chapter Eight

Bryce stood in front of Ms. Medley's door trying to find the strength to go through with the plan. After talking himself out of it at least a dozen times, he finally lifted his hand and knocked softly on the door. *Please God, don't let her answer and I'll never ask you for anything ever again,* he thought to himself.

When the door flew open a few seconds later, Bryce couldn't believe his eyes. Ms. Medley stood with a silk, floral printed robe that resembled a shower curtain. He felt his stomach turn when she raised her arm to lean against the door frame posing like she was the next Playboy Playmate.

To make matters worse, Ms. Medley had on black, fish net thigh high stockings that had bulges of fat poking out of each open space. Her black panties which seemed extremely dingy had garter belts that connected to the stockings. With her massive breasts hanging down in a tight camisole, Bryce was even more disgusted looking at her thimble sized nipples protruding out.

She resembled a grazing cow as her mouth opened and closed chewing on what had to be an entire pack of gum. *I can't believe my wife signed me up for this shit,* Bryce said to himself.

Overly excited, Ms. Medley snatched Bryce into her apartment, slammed the door, then blocked it with her enormous frame. Bryce swallowed the large lump in his throat when she began rubbing her breasts with both hands.

"Umm…I think there's been a big mistake. Whatever you have in mind I don't think that was part of the deal," Bryce said.

"Oh my darling, I think you were told the wrong thing. Me and your wife had an agreement. I offered to forget about the rent and credit next month's rent only if you left me fully satisfied. I would hate to evict you and that wife of yours because you didn't honor our agreement. How do you think your wife will react to my son throwin' all your shit out on the curb?" Ms. Medley answered.

Bryce seemed confused. "What was the agreement you had with my wife?"

"The agreement was for me to feel that big, thick dick pounding deep inside this pussy until I cum so hard I can barely breathe," Ms. Medley replied.

Bryce's eyes enlarged. "Well, you might as well get that thought out your fucking head. It ain't no way I'm doing anything close to that with you."

"You better call your fuckin' wife right now. If I'm not happy then the entire deal is off. That was her guarantee when we shook hands on it."

Taking out his phone, Bryce quickly dialed Seven's number. The phone rang a couple of times before she finally answered. "Yes, my love."

"What the fuck did you agree to? Ms. Medley just told me that she's expecting me to fuck her in order to squash our debt. You told me that all I had to do was keep her company. I know you didn't lie to me and promise this woman any sexual contact on my behalf in your little deal!" Bryce shouted angrily.

"Calm down. I knew if I told you the truth you would never do it, so yes I did lie. Look, it's either that or us out on the fucking street. You promised that you would take care of me. Live up to your end of the fucking bargain," Seven snapped.

Bryce turned his back toward Ms. Medley and whispered

into the phone. "I can't have sex with her. My dick wouldn't even get hard. You should see her."

"I know you can do it. I have faith in you and your love for me. Just close your eyes and visualize me in my white silk teddy. Feel my soft, milky skin touching you and my luscious lips kissing you as you make love to me over and over again," Seven moaned.

"I can't!" Bryce yelled into the phone.

Suddenly Seven's attitude changed. "Okay, but know this. I won't live on the fucking streets. It's either you handle your business or don't bother coming upstairs because nothing will be waiting for you when you get here!" she yelled before hanging up.

Bryce turned around to find Ms. Medley standing fully naked in front of the door. Seeing all the rolls and dimples made his stomach turn along with the hair growing on parts of her body that God never intended for women to possess.

"I don't think I can do this Ms. Medley," Bryce said hanging up his phone.

"Call me Phyllis."

"Alright Phyllis. Why don't we just sit and talk? Let's just end this night on a good note. We can have a wonderful time doing something else, anything else," he pleaded.

"Take your fuckin' clothes off so I can feel that dick inside me," she demanded.

Bryce stood frozen. As bad as he wanted to knock her down and haul ass back upstairs, his thoughts immediately went to visions of Seven packing up and leaving him. He looked around at her nasty apartment with empty takeout containers tossed everywhere and ashtrays filled with cigarette butts.

God, please help me get through this shit, he thought.

Stepping over several shoes and magazines, Bryce made his way to the couch then slowly did as he was instructed by removing his clothes. When he dropped his boxers, Phyllis started clapping with excitement. She looked just like the mother from *The Nutty Professor* movie.

"I knew you had a big dick. This is gonna be a night neither one of us will ever forget," Phyllis said walking toward him.

Bryce quickly tried to do what Seven told him. He closed his eyes and tried to envision her walking over to him in sexy lingerie, but it still had no effect on his dick. All he could concentrate on was the loud thumps of Phyllis' feet punishing the carpet underneath with each step. Bryce's dick hung limp as his thoughts of Seven still couldn't arouse him to an erection. With Phyllis' heavy breathing getting closer, he didn't know what to do.

"Would you like a drink to settle your nerves?" Phyllis asked.

"Bring me the fucking bottle," Bryce replied. *I'ma need to get fucked up for this.*

Phyllis walked over to her kitchen and grabbed a bottle of Thunderbird off the counter with one hand and two glasses that looked like empty mayonnaise jars with the other. She had a huge smile on her face as she turned to face Bryce.

Handing Bryce his glass, Phyllis quickly filled it up with the cheap wine, then watched as Bryce turned it up to his mouth and swallowed it all in one straight gulp. Bryce motioned with his hand for her to fill him up again.

"I love a man after he's been drinkin', but you're no good to me passed out on my couch," she said, pouring him another drink.

Bryce quickly gulped the wine down just like the first one. "I'll be alright."

When Phyllis sat down next to him, she reached her hand out to take the glass, but Bryce pleaded for just one more. This time she only filled the third glass half way.

"I've been wantin' to fuck you every since you moved in here. I couldn't believe that a man like you would live in such a place with a woman like your wife," Phyllis said. tracing her lips with her large, thick tongue.

"This was only supposed to be for a year so we could

save up a down payment for a house of our own."

"I'm so glad your plan didn't work out," she replied blowing him a kiss.

Bryce tossed back the third drink when he saw Phyllis raise one of her humongous breasts then start to lick her nipple. *It's no way I'm kissing this bitch*, he thought.

"Would you like for me to spark up some weed? I can roll us a blunt if you get high. I have some shit that'll really take the edge off."

"I don't smoke, but if you want to get your smoke on, don't let me stop you," Bryce replied hoping that would buy him some time.

"I was just tryin' to help you out," Phyllis responded. "In that case, I'm ready to take this party into my bedroom where we can get wild."

Bryce envisioned the death row march as he grabbed his pants and allowed her to pull him toward the bedroom. The further they went into the apartment, the messier it got. However from her constant nasty appearance, Bryce wasn't surprised she lived that way. What he was surprised about was the fifty inch flat screen T.V. on her bedroom wall, which didn't go with the rest of the place.

"Can you please turn off the lights and put the television on some kind of game. I last longer when I'm watching sports," Bryce said, knowing that a game would do just the opposite. Bryce moved a plate with half eaten pasta salad from the king sized bed and dropped it on the floor right before laying down.

"Okay I did everything you asked, now let's go mutha-fucka. Let's see if you can handle a real woman," Phyllis said laying down beside him.

Bryce slowly crawled off the bed down to the floor, slid a condom on his dick that was in his pants pocket, then took position between Phyllis' legs. He lifted her ass cheeks then tickled his limp dick between her pussy lips. *I can't believe what I'm about to do for the sake of money,* he thought.

Trying desperately to think of his wife's amazing body

again, as soon as his dick got hard, Bryce rammed his tool into Phyllis' dripping pussy. His dick banged against her walls causing a sensational pain, and also caused Phyllis to let out a loud moan that sent chills up her body. Suddenly, a frown appeared on Bryce's face when a foul odor reached his nostrils.

What the fuck is that, he wondered. Thinking it couldn't be anything else other than her pussy, Bryce placed his left hand over his mouth and nose to block the smell. He began to feel sick to his stomach as his body continued to jerk in and out of her moistening vagina. He needed this to be over.

Bryce pushed with deeper thrusts, then decided to pick up the pace, hoping the end was near. Phyllis cried out in enjoyment as Bryce pounded her nest until her legs became weak. Moments later, he leaned back on his heels and watched as she shook uncontrollably from her powerful orgasm. He didn't mind the fact that she'd cum and he didn't. All he wanted to do was go home.

Chapter **Nine**

"So, how did it go?" Seven asked when Bryce walked through the door. She was smiling from ear to ear. "I could hear her yelling down there."

Still freaked out from the whole experience, Bryce didn't say a word. Instead, he went straight to the bathroom and turned on the shower. As the foul smell of Phyllis' pussy still lingered in his nostrils, Bryce snatched his clothes off in record time and stepped into the tub. Feeling completely dirty, he scrubbed with all his might trying to get Phyllis' sweat off of his skin. In his entire thirty-two years, this had to be the most degrading and embarrassing thing he'd ever done. Now Bryce knew he had to think of another plan for the money because the escort idea definitely wasn't going to work out. Deep in thought, Bryce didn't even realize that the shower curtain had been pulled back, until he heard Seven's voice.

"Didn't you hear me when you first came in? How did it go? I need the details," she said, bouncing up and down like a toddler in line for the ice-cream truck. "I wanna know everything. What positions did you put her big ass in? Did you remember to use a condom? I know you wore a condom right?" Seven badgered.

"I really don't want to talk about it right now," Bryce replied. Answering her questions, would've made him relive the ordeal all over again. "Can you close the curtain? It's a little cold."

Seven decided not to push him. "Okay, you don't have to tell me right now. I just want you to know that this gesture has really shown me how much you love me. I love you for trying to make things happen for us."

Bryce stuck his head out and gave Seven a deep, passionate kiss. For once he felt appreciated.

Bryce was awakened by the alarm clock blasting in his ears instead of his normal sexual routine with Seven. After turning off the annoying device, he rolled over, then felt up and down the cold sheets for his wife. When he didn't feel anything, Bryce opened his eyes, realizing that she'd already gotten up.

Bryce stared at the ceiling still remembering moments from last night's adventure. Looking back on it, he couldn't believe that he'd let Seven talk him into something like that. But what was even more mind boggling was the fact that she was so comfortable with him fucking another woman, especially a big, fat, nasty one like Phyllis. Now, he was ready to discuss it.

"Seven!" Bryce called out to no reply.

Looking back at the clock, it was only 6:30 a.m. so he knew she hadn't left for work yet. Just when he was about to call her name again, Bryce glanced over at the bedroom door as Seven emerged from the hallway carrying a tray with Eggo waffles, eggs, and apple sauce.

"Good morning, the love of my life. I made you breakfast," she said with a huge smile.

Completely stunned, Bryce watched as Seven held the tray like a proud chef. She'd never made him breakfast in bed before. "Who are you, and what have you done with my wife?" he asked. She probably thought he was joking, but he was dead serious.

"Oh, be quiet silly. Come on…sit up before this gets

cold."

"So, what's this all about?" he asked following her orders.

Seven placed the tray over Bryce's lap. "This is just my way of saying thank you once again for stepping up to the plate last night."

Bryce appreciated her sincere tone, but he was still curious about a few things. "How could you tell Phyllis that sex was part of the deal? You could've at least asked me what I felt comfortable doing before putting me out there like that."

"Who is Phyllis?"

"That's Ms. Medley's first name. Now, answer the question."

Seven seemed pissed that Bryce wasn't as excited as she was. "Look, we do what we have to in order to survive."

"How did you know that I would go through with it? I mean that was some really fucked up shit for you to do. I thought I was just gonna be escorting women to events and maybe a few dinner dates, but fucking 'em. I still can't believe you're this comfortable with that."

"Don't think of it like that. Phyllis and anyone else is just a means to an end, our end. Besides, how much money do you think we'll make with you only going on dates? You'll get way more for taking it to the next level."

"I feel so disgusted. I can't stop replaying last night over in my head and her nasty smell won't seem to go away," Bryce said in a stern voice. "Maybe since you were a dancer and not an escort, it's hard for you to understand."

Seven felt guilty for a moment, but quickly dismissed it. She leaned over and kissed Bryce's forehead. "It'll fade, trust me. You're thinking way too much about it. She was just a toy added into a night of kinky sex... nothing more. If you think of her and any other woman in that way, you'll be fine."

"What? Who are you right now? This conversation is starting to piss me off."

Seven went in her pocket and pulled out fifty dollars.

"Well maybe you should calm down because this is your tip from last night. Phyllis actually knocked on the door while I was cooking to give it to me. Now, if she's up this early you must've really put it on her last night, which is what I've been trying to tell you all along. These women are gonna go crazy for you. Don't worry, everything is gonna work out. Now, eat your food," she said kissing Bryce on the top of his head. "I'll even take you to work today."

He watched as Seven turned around and left the room, never bothering to give him his share of the money.

Several days went by with Bryce noticing that Seven had a different bounce in her step. She wasn't complaining, fussing about minor things or arguing with him over everything missing in her life. She'd replaced all of that with cleaning the house, cooking meals and catering to his every sexual need. When Bryce thought about it, their sex had been incredible lately. Over the past few months, Seven only liked to have sex in the morning, but now she'd turned into an animal, wanting it every-day and in every possible position. Bryce even got text messages throughout the day with Seven expressing her love for him. He couldn't believe how fucking Phyllis had strengthened their marriage, but for some strange reason it seemed to be doing just that.

Bryce returned home from work one evening to find Seven on the phone watching television. She had an amazing glow on her face as she wrote on a notepad and answered "not a problem," into the receiver.

"Hey baby," Bryce said closing the door.

"I have to go now. Everything will be in place for Saturday night. Satisfaction is my number one guarantee," Seven replied to the caller before hanging up. "Hi baby, how was your day at work?" She wrote one last thing down, then turned to look at Bryce.

"My day was cool. Darrell asks me about that down payment every time I see him."

"So that means we need to get this money, huh?"

"I guess," Bryce replied, walking into the kitchen to find dinner on the stove.

"Well, I've been working my ass off to set us up for that," Seven said following him.

Bryce picked up a fork to taste the red beans and rice. "You're kidding right," he said with a mouth full of food.

"Let's not go through this again. You want something and you know this is the only way of getting that," Seven responded.

"I was really hoping that this shit would be a one time thing. After being with Phyllis I don't think I can go through with it."

"So, do you know a better way for us to get this money then? Why are you tripping over having to fuck other women if I'm alright with the idea? You seem to be having all these fucking issues. Most men would be happy to be in your situation. You have a free pass, and you're still complaining."

"Seven this shit isn't as easy as it seems."

"I bet if I brought Halle Berry up in this bitch, you'd change your mind."

Bryce couldn't help but smile. "Honey, I'm just afraid that this is gonna come between us."

"The only way this will come between us is if you start fucking bitches that aren't paying or going on dates that I didn't set up. I'm being very selective by choosing women who I know won't damage us. It's a win – win situation," Seven said.

Bryce paused for a moment. "Promise me that if I go along with this, you won't let shit get out of hand." He walked over to his wife and placed his arms around her.

"I promise honey. Now, sit down so we can go over the rules you need to follow."

"Rules?" Bryce questioned as he sat next to Seven at the small kitchen table. "Okay, tell me what you've been working on."

When she handed him the paper, Bryce was shocked when he realized that Seven had actually typed up a list and had it printed out.

1. You are never allowed to go on a date that has not been set up or approved by me.

2. You are never allowed to leave a client unsatisfied.

3. You must always wear a condom whenever having sex.

4. You must always inform me whenever a client wants something extra on the date.

5. You must never kiss a client on the lips, especially French kissing (too intimate).

6. You must never tell a client that you are my husband. (We need them to feel comfortable).

7. You must never allow a client to pay less than $300.00 for simple escort dates and a separate $500.00 fee for sex.

8. You must agree that all money made will go to bills first, then into a savings account.

9. You must never keep a secret from me about a client. ***You must allow me to manage all monies made.

"So, can you can handle all those things?" Seven asked when Bryce finally put the paper down.

"Of course. Nothing seems too hard," Bryce replied. "But why are there asterisks beside number ten?"

"Because that's the most important rule. Obviously if you handle the money, we might end up in the same position."

"You got a point," he agreed.

"Good. Now, let's stop playing and go get this money. I've set up something easy for this weekend just to baby step our way to the bigger paydays."

"What do I have to do?"

"Well, you'll be escorting a woman named Angelique to a welcoming party at her law firm. Angelique represents several professional athletes and she just moved up here from Dallas. She wants to use your services as a pretend boyfriend so it can take some of the heat off her being single in a male dominated field. Trust me this time. All she wants is a simple escort. She didn't pay for anything extra."

"I can't believe women actually pay for dates," Bryce said followed with a small laugh. *I bet she's ugly as shit if she can't find a man*, he thought. "Since this is only an escort. I'm positive I can handle this one with no problem," he added then tapped his chest.

Seven smiled. "Enough about that, are you ready for your dinner?"

"Sure."

Bryce watched as his beautiful wife fixed their plates. Minutes later Seven sat down at the table with two glasses of iced tea and a slice of red velvet cake for them to share.

"There's no way you fixed this," Bryce said, putting a piece of cornbread in his mouth.

"Shit, I wish. Maybe one day I'll learn how to cook like an old woman," she said. "No, I went to Two Sisters on my way home."

"Well, thank you for picking dinner up. It's delicious."

Seven smiled. "Nothing is too good for my man. As a matter of fact, I got another surprise for you in the bedroom." She stood up and extended her hand. "Come on."

"But I'm still eating," Bryce replied.

"So, make up your mind. Would you rather eat that or..." Seven paused, patting her pussy, "this."

Bryce immediately dropped his fork.

BEDROOM GANGSTA

Chapter Ten

Bryce called the number Seven had given him to let Angelique know he was driving into the Warehouse District. Her voice sounded very seductive which damn near confirmed his thoughts about how she looked. The sexier the voice usually meant the uglier the woman. Once he pulled up in front of the chic condominium, Bryce parked right out front. Trying to be the perfect gentleman, he got out, walked around to the passenger side and opened the door. Bryce stood there looking at the craftsmanship of the new high-rise building called Tracage and thought, *I can't wait to see this broad.*

He couldn't wait to see what monstrosity would emerge from the double glass doors. However, when the doors opened a few moments later, Bryce had to catch himself from drooling. With long firm legs that seemed to never end, Angelique looked stunning in a cream Herve Leger bandage dress. A dress that left very little room for his imagination. Her hour glass figure poked out in all the right places. He watched as her long black weave that was parted down the middle blew in the light September wind with each step. The glow from her smooth caramel skin even seemed to glisten. Bryce was stunned by her beauty.

A woman that fine with no man must be incredibly psycho, he thought watching her strut toward the car.

"You must be Bryce," Angelique said walking up.

"Yes," Bryce answered as his eyes traced her body.

She smiled. "It's a pleasure to meet you. I hope Seven told you about what we're getting ready to do. I need for this to go really smooth so I can get the guys at the firm off my back."

Bryce nodded and continued to stare.

"Is there a problem?"

"Oh, no. It's just that you're not what I expected. I was imagining Fiona from Shrek to be waiting for me," Bryce admitted.

"I'll take that as a compliment," Angelique said, sliding past Bryce and getting into the car.

"I need the address so I can plug it into my Tom Tom," Bryce said once he got into the drivers seat.

Angelique looked over at Bryce. "You know what, why don't we drive my car? The guys at the firm will think they have a chance if we pulled up in this," Angelique said with a slight chuckle. "No offense though."

"None taken. I'm sure those fake ass lawyers will think that regardless of what we pull up in. But this is your date and I'm here to be at your every beck and call," Bryce responded.

"That's true, but I still know these type of people better than you, so we'll take my car. Besides I'm worried about how well you will do when the conversations start with the members of the firm and my partners."

"Don't worry about me. I can handle myself. I'm not some stupid idiot who's gonna embarrass you," Bryce shot back. *Damn, she's fine, but I hope she's not a bitch,* he thought.

After telling him where to park Seven's car, Bryce followed Angelique to the parking garage where she walked toward a black Mercedes S550. He admired her twenty-one inch rims and Pirelli tires. Bryce started to walk around to the passenger side when Angelique held out the keys.

"You better not scratch my ride," she said.

Bryce's face lit up like he'd won the lottery. He kept his cool while strolling over and taking the keys from Angelique's hand. "I'll be extra careful with this amazing machine," he said.

Driving off, Angelique spent the entire ride informing Bryce of all the smallest details just in case a partner pinned him up in the corner. False details like how and where they'd met, where he supposedly worked, and their plans for the future.

"Do you really think it's gonna be that intense? I thought this was your welcoming party. The focus will be on you, not me," Bryce said when Angelique paused long enough for him to get a word in.

"I haven't discussed my relationship status with anyone at the firm. It's going to be a major deal when we walk into that party. Trust me when I say this has to be perfect, all the way down to the color of lipgloss that I prefer," Angelique replied.

Bryce stared as her tongue traced the perimeter of her pink colored lips. At that moment he could feel his dick growing between his legs. He quickly reflected back to Angelique's last statement about being able to handle her co-workers. Bryce really wasn't worried about anything Angelique said because he knew that he could hold his own with all types of people. Yet when they pulled up into the parking garage of the law firm, he felt a sense of nervousness rush over his body.

The firm went all out for Angelique. They'd hired the best caterers, balloons that spelled out welcome, an assortment of wine and top shelf liquors. Bryce smiled when he realized most of the men were straight out of a Tom Cruise movie. They all wore black or navy blue tailored made suits, Prada loafers and laughed at the exact same time.

Bryce felt all eyes fall upon him and Angelique as they strolled around the room. He remembered to shake hands firmly, spoke in a commanding tone, then quickly gave his full attention right back to Angelique.

"So, you're the lucky guy," an older, white man asked walking up.

"Bryce, let me introduce you to Mr. Covington. Mr. Covington this is my boyfriend Bryce," Angelique stated. "He's a senior partner here at Sloan, Covington & King," Angelique said to Bryce.

"I think he could've figured that out when he heard my name and saw it written on everything around here," Mr. Covington sarcastically replied.

"It's nice to meet you and yes, you're right, I am a lucky guy," Bryce answered.

"Angelique, Mr. King needs to ask you something before the party really gets started. I'll keep Bryce company," Mr. Covington informed.

Angelique's eyes bounced back and forth from Mr. Covington to Bryce. She felt a nervous weight press down on her chest as she leaned over to kiss Bryce on the lips. "You behave yourself," Angelique said. She grabbed a glass of champagne on her way over toward Mr. King and downed it. She was obviously nervous.

The kiss took Bryce by surprise. The first thing that came to his mind was the rule that prohibited him from kissing. The second thought was how soft and sweet her lips were. *It was just a quick little peck*, Bryce said to himself. *Seven shouldn't be mad at that.*

"Let's go get a drink," Mr. Covington said smacking Bryce on the shoulder.

Bryce kept glancing back at Angelique as he walked toward one of the fully stocked bars. When he saw the major worry on her face, Bryce flashed a little smile to assure Angelique that everything would be okay. By the time she was finished talking several minutes later, Bryce and Mr. Covington were nowhere to be found. Angelique walked around the office for a few moments before finally hearing a loud, boisterous laugh coming from the middle of the courtyard. She walked over, looked out the window and saw the majority of the men from her firm laughing with Bryce like they were all old friends. Feeling a sense of relief, Angelique walked over and took position by his side.

"Angelique, you must bring Bryce around more often," Mr. Sloan said still laughing.

Angelique looked over at Bryce. She realized how sexy

he really was at that very moment. With an impressed look on her face, Angelique grabbed Bryce's arm. "I guess you weren't lying when you said I didn't have to worry because you could handle yourself," she whispered.

Bryce winked his eye. "Told you."

The remainder of the night went smooth with Bryce charming the pants off of everyone he talked with. The men treated Bryce like one of the boys while the women constantly smiled at him like he was a present under the Christmas tree. It had been a successful evening.

Downing several more glasses of champagne, Angelique had a little buzz by the time they drove back to her condo. "I owe you everything," she said to Bryce. "I don't know how or what you did, but it sure worked. You had everyone eating out the palm of your hand."

"Well I'm sure when you hired me you expected a certain level of service, so I didn't want to disappoint," Bryce replied.

Looking at his sexy lips move, Angelique started to get horny all of a sudden. Her thoughts went back to Seven telling her about the prices for any sexual contact. She leaned back into her plush leather seat and closed her eyes. *I wonder if he's as good in bed as he is in everything else*, she thought. When they pulled up to her building a few minutes later, Angelique looked over at him with lustful eyes. It was definitely clear that she wanted something a little extra.

"Hey, I have an idea. Why don't you come inside for a drink? I really wanna see what you have to offer in the bedroom."

Caught completely off guard, Bryce didn't know how to respond especially since changing services mid-date was one of the rules.

"Umm…that sounds good, but I need to call my…" He was about to break yet another rule. "I need to call Seven first. She's strict about knowing everything that goes on."

"Oh, yeah that would be the best thing to do. She seems

pretty strict. Can I ask you a question?"

"Sure."

"How did you get into this line of work and how do you know Seven? She seemed really overprotective of you over the phone."

Bryce didn't know her question would be personal. "We're really good friends and it's a long story."

Angelique could tell that he was uncomfortable. "I'll tell you what, we can call her in the house. Is that okay with you?"

Bryce felt extremely pressured. "Yeah, that's cool I guess."

Following her into the building and up to the seventieth floor, Bryce was in awe of her place when Angelique opened the door. With floor to ceiling windows, she had an amazing view of the Mississippi River and the Garden District. Bryce went to sit on the couch as Angelique locked the door and dialed Seven's phone number. The call went straight to voice mail.

"I need to charge up my phone. I'll call her from the house phone in my bedroom," Angelique informed.

Bryce wasn't sure if he should follow her or wait in the living room. Moments later, he heard his name being called from off in the distance. He slowly got off the couch and began walking toward Angelique's voice. When he got to the bedroom, she was laying on the bed completely naked. Bryce stood frozen as he admired the firm silhouette of her 5'9 frame, and perfect thirty-six C breasts.

"The best thing about having you on the payroll is no small talk, no cuddling afterwards and especially no fucking awkward feelings when you get up and leave," Angelique said. "Now, I want you to take off those damn clothes and handle your business."

Bryce didn't respond. He stood there wondering if she'd gotten in touch with Seven about taking the date further. Bryce couldn't take his eyes off how sexy she looked as Angelique used her hands to explore every inch of her body. He was hesitant at first, but quickly decided that Seven would be pissed if he didn't make the extra money, so he stepped further into her bedroom.

Luckily, I have an emergency condom in my wallet, he thought, then pulled it out.

Once he removed his clothes, Bryce walked over to the bed and took position down on his knees. Bryce kept his eyes lowered not to make any eye contact as he slowly opened Angelique's legs and began kissing her vagina. The sweet taste of her pussy along with Angelique's gentle hands rubbing across the top of his head quickly made him speed up the pace. He devoured her as if she was his last meal on death row.

Over the next few minutes, Bryce treated her body with extra care paying close attention to every part. Once the oral session was over, Bryce quickly placed the condom on, then dove straight in her nest with his shaft. The moans and screams grew louder as they experimented with several positions. Angelique's pussy was so good that he felt an early orgasm approaching. Bryce tried to fight it off, but realized that he was enjoying her body just a little too much. He felt guilty that his thoughts were really of Angelique and not Seven, or a faceless toy that his wife had suggested.

When he couldn't take it anymore, Bryce pulled out, yanked the condom off and finally released a large barrage of thick cum all over Angelique's breasts. His dick began to weaken until she began to massage his juices all over her chest. With a sudden burst of new energy, Bryce went to put his uncovered shaft back inside Angelique's dripping pussy, but at the last moment decided to switch gears. Suddenly, he made his way back between her legs, then licked up her juices with his tongue causing Angelique to let out one final scream.

Within seconds, Angelique's legs started to shake hysterically. She stretched one of her hands up and pressed against the head board, using the other hand to caress her body. Just as exhausted, Bryce fell onto his back. He started to rub his head questioning if he was supposed to enjoy the sex that much. Bryce also didn't know if it was wrong that he was comparing this to some of the best pussy he'd ever had.

"That was amazing," Angelique said.

Bryce didn't want to hear anything else. He was already feeling bad enough. He jumped up and started putting on his clothes, keeping his head down the entire time.

"Is something wrong?"

"Nothing, I just gotta go."

"Well, I already put the money by the door," Angelique replied. "Sorry I didn't give you the original $300 when the date first started. Seven strongly expressed that when we talked."

Bryce finally glanced up at her. Looking at her sexy body, several thoughts ran through his head that he knew shouldn't. Before he got in trouble, Bryce rushed to put on the rest of his clothes and headed for the door. He paused, looking back at how beautiful Angelique was. Bryce rubbed his face as if to erase her from his memory before snatching the money and hurrying out of the door.

Bryce walked into the house half an hour later to find Seven waiting for him on the couch again. When he gave her a white envelope, her face lit up with excitement.

"What do we have here?" she asked.

"It's the money from Angelique."

When Seven pulled out the crisp, ten hundred dollar bills. her smile instantly faded. "Hold up...this is a thousand dollars. She was only supposed to pay you three hundred. So, you mean to tell me that you got a seven hundred dollar tip?" she inquired.

At that moment, Bryce realized that Angelique hadn't gotten in touch with Seven after all. "Umm…"

"Umm what?" Seven asked in a stern tone.

"There's probably a two hundred dollar tip in there for me, but the other five hundred came from us having sex."

Seven's eyes increased. "What? Did you just say that y'all had sex?" When Bryce nodded his head, she went off. "What the fuck do you mean y'all had sex? Didn't you agree to the rules?" Before he could answer, Seven ran to their bedroom and came back out with the list. "Number fucking four. You must inform me whenever a client wants something extra on the date!" Seven read off the paper.

"We tried to call you honey, but you didn't answer," Bryce said in a low tone. He hoped like hell she would check her phone to see the missed call. "I would never break the rules. I promise."

Trying to calm down, Seven threw the list, then picked the envelope full of money back up. This time she realized there was also a handwritten note inside.

Thanks for the wonderful evening. I will definitely recommend your services.

Love,

Angelique.

"Well, I guess you made one hell of an impression once again," Seven said, recounting the money for the second time.

Bryce felt uneasy at how the sight of money earned from fucking another woman obviously aroused his wife. She'd calmed down way too fast. Moments later, Seven finally asked him about the date, but Bryce just shrugged his shoulder and went to take a shower.

As the warm water ran down his back, Bryce imagined Angelique's naked body and her sweet sexual juices. *Man, get yourself together before this shit gets out of hand,* he thought.

Chapter Eleven

Bryce woke up from his sleep when several plastic bags hit him in the face. Instantly opening his eyes, he was surprised to see a variety of department store bags laying all around him. When Bryce finally sat up, Seven was standing at the foot of the bed smiling.

"What's all this?" he asked with a confused expression.

"Open 'em up!" Seven shouted like it was his birthday.

Bryce first opened the Macy's bag to find several new dress shirts along with a few ties. Not knowing what to say, he just sat there in disbelief.

"Open this one next," Seven commanded.

As soon as Bryce opened the bag and saw the Ferragamo box, he knew it was a pair of shoes. This time his face tightened.

"Do you like them?" Seven asked.

Bryce shrugged his shoulders. "I guess."

"You guess? Those are $500.00 loafers that I got on sale for $235.00. Feel the leather, they're not just a regular pair of dress shoes." She seemed offended.

"You spent over two hundred dollars for a pair of dress shoes. Are you high? We have bills out the ass and you're running around buying new shit. I thought we decided that all the money would go to bills first, then savings."

"Look, I haven't forgot about the bills. But you gotta

spend money to make money," Seven replied tossing a little box toward him.

"You bought more shit?" he asked.

"It's just some smell good, but don't worry about the cost. What you need to worry about is the time. I've booked you a major client and time is ticking. She needs your services in an urgent sort of way."

"Seven, it's Monday. Did you forget that I have a job?"

"Don't worry about that either. I took care of everything. I already called and told your boss that you weren't feeling well and wouldn't be in today. The money we're getting from this one job is more than what you'd make at that bullshit ass garage today anyway. Trust me baby, we can't pass this client up, so I need you to hurry up and shower because her husband will be home around two o'clock this afternoon," Seven said turning to walk out the room.

Bryce couldn't be in more shock. "What? Are you crazy? Why the hell would you set me up with a married woman? I'm not comfortable with that."

"Because her money is green and spends like everybody else's."

"Come on, Seven. There's gotta be a limit to this shit," Bryce said.

"If it doesn't interfere with our rules, then everything else is fair game," Seven proudly stated. "Now, come on. I started the shower, so you need to get a move on."

"Why would you want to break up a happy home just to make some money?" Bryce continued.

"The home can't be all that fucking happy if she's using your services," Seven fired back. "Now, can you please stop whining? Why is this so fucking hard?"

"Because she's married, that's why. I'm not going."

At that moment, Seven gave him a look of death. "I'm not gonna keep arguing with you every time I set up a date. Either you're gonna start doing this minus all these bullshit morals and complaints or we can call everything off and you can get the fuck out."

Once again Bryce was speechless. "The fact that you would put me out just because I don't wanna be with a married woman is crazy."

"Well then, I'll leave. I can call my brother right now. The bottom line is, I'm tired of fucking struggling, so either you're gonna do this or not."

Bryce thought about it for a second. He did feel bad for putting Seven in their financial situation, and for not taking care of her the way he'd promised. In actuality she deserved the best, and since he was responsible for making that happen, Bryce was willing to do whatever it took to make her happy.

"So, where does this woman live?" he asked with apologetic eyes.

Bryce slowly drove down English Turn Drive, which ironically was the same street he'd visited the night he got drunk. Exploring the expensive neighborhood, his head went back and forth scanning each home for the client's address. After finally finding the right house, he pulled up into the long circular driveway, eying the sixty-four hundred square foot mansion. Still feeling uneasy about her being married, Bryce was glad the driveway went all the way around just in case he had to make a prompt escape.

"I need to make this shit quick," he said getting out of the car.

Walking up the cobblestone steps, Bryce pressed the doorbell and waited. Moments later, he could see the silhouette of a person walking through the frosted glass door.

When the door finally opened, Bryce was completely shocked. The woman standing in front of him had the face of a child, but that wasn't the cause of his reaction. She had to be about seven or eight months pregnant on top of that. *Please don't let this be the client*, he thought.

"Are you Bryce?" she asked.

"Yes, are you Alicia?"

"Yes I am. You need to hurry up and come inside before one of my nosey neighbors sees you," she replied. "Where would you prefer to do this?" she asked closing the door behind him. She was obviously ready to get down to business.

"Umm, I…I don't know. Are you sure we can do something in your condition?" Bryce questioned with concern.

"Yes. I want to teach my husband that two can play the same game. He thinks just because he's rich and I'm twenty-five years younger than him, he can just treat me like shit. Well, I'm not the one. I'm gonna let you fuck me while I'm pregnant with his child."

Bryce glanced over at a picture of an elderly gentleman and Alicia on the foyer table. "Is that your husband?"

"Yeah, that's his cheating ass. He's coming back in town today after spending three days in the Bahamas with his white, blond haired mistress. Every time I think about that shit, it turns me off, so fuck him. Come on, let's get this going," Alicia said pulling Bryce by the arm.

Bryce followed Alicia to a bedroom at the end of the hall on the second level. When they walked inside, the room reminded him of something from a MTV Cribs episode. With everything inside resembling a luxury furniture store showroom, Bryce was afraid to touch anything since he couldn't afford to pay for it if it broke.

Alicia handed him a stack of cash that appeared to be all hundreds. "That's for your services."

"Oh, thanks," he said, stuffing the money into the front pocket of his jeans.

Bryce couldn't stop thinking about what he and Alicia were about to do as he stared at her watermelon sized stomach. He also couldn't stop staring at the beautiful glow her skin had. He wondered if Seven would still be that pretty whenever she became pregnant. Slipping out of his thoughts, he watched as Alicia took off her grey, ruched maternity dress and crawled onto the bed. It was weird seeing her naked body. Bryce took off his clothes, piled them up near the door, then grabbed a condom. He walked closer to the bed before massaging his dick so it was nice and hard by the time they were ready for business.

"Do you think you can make it darker in here?" Bryce asked hoping not to see her protruding belly while they fucked.

"Sure."

Alicia reached over and grabbed a remote control off of the night stand. She then pressed a button which caused the custom made curtains to slowly close. Even though the room was darker, Bryce could still see her clearly as he layed down next to her. When Alicia began kissing his chest, she quickly nudged his hand to go toward her pussy.

Bryce slid his hand down, but became hesitant when he got near her stomach. It tickled Alicia as his fingers ran across her belly like a spider. When Bryce finally made his way between her thighs, Alicia's pussy was extremely wet.

This may not be that bad, he thought.

"Oh, that feels so good. I haven't been with another man in years. I really need this," Alicia said.

Bryce began shaking Alicia's clit until her sex juices were dripping off his hand. Knowing she was beyond ready, he got on top of her, then slowly eased his swollen dick into her vagina. Instead of banging, Bryce found a steady pace and kept it at that speed as he moved in and out. Bryce would only slide a portion of his dick inside Alicia out of fear of hurting the baby. However, every now and then Alicia would try and force Bryce to pound on top of her. He even held his body up in the air so he wouldn't touch her stomach. But he had to admit, Alicia's nest was super moist and gripped his dick perfectly. He wondered if all pregnant pussy felt that way.

I'm going to bang the shit out of Seven when she's in this condition. If I would've known pregnant women felt this good, I would've knocked Seven up a long time ago, he thought.

As if she'd had enough of his nonsense, Alicia suddenly pushed Bryce off of her before jumping on top of him. Riding his dick like a Texas Rodeo champion, Alicia moved her body up and down at a rapid pace until she experienced a strong orgasm. When Alicia tried to repeat the same process, Bryce lifted his legs so he could control how far she bounced on his shaft. It took a little longer, but she still managed to have a second orgasm several minutes later. He wasn't even interested in cumming. As long as she'd gotten hers, that's all that mattered.

Alicia rolled off of Bryce. After trying to catch her breath, it appeared as if she wanted to have a bit of pillow talk when suddenly the sound of an engine pulling up into the driveway startled her. Her eyes widened as she hopped up, walked toward the window and peeked through the curtains to find her husband getting out of his chauffer driven Town Car.

"Oh my God! It's my husband. He's early!" Alicia yelled before covering her mouth with her hand.

"What? I knew this shit was gonna happen!" Bryce replied.

He frantically jumped out of the bed and ran over to his clothes.

"Okay, we need a plan," Alicia said, putting her dress back on. She then started pacing the floor.

"I need to get the fuck outta here, that's the plan!" he barked.

Within moments, they heard the alarm chime. "Alicia, where are you? Who's car is outside?" her husband yelled.

Bryce's heart felt like it was in his throat. "Shit!"

"Sshh…I got it." She pointed to the other side of the room. "Go get into the walk-in closet and I'll take care of the rest."

"Are you crazy? People always get caught in the fucking closet. What are you gonna do?" Bryce questioned. Still, he allowed her to quickly push him to the other side of the room.

"He likes to have sex in our upstairs office, so I'm gonna take him in there so he'll think that's what's about to go down. I'll leave this bedroom door open so when you hear me slam the other door, that's the signal for you to sneak out," Alicia instructed just before pushing Bryce inside.

Bryce continued to get dressed with his ear near the door. He could hear her husband asking once again whose car was outside, and Alicia telling him that it belonged to her cousin, who he's never met. She also told him that her cousin would be by to pick the car up at any moment. Bryce hoped like hell that her husband would believe the ridiculous lie. Just as he was putting on his shoes, suddenly he heard a door slam shut. Hoping that was his cue, Bryce took off out the closet, tip-toed down the stairs, and raced to his car.

Bryce didn't even look back as he pulled out the driveway. He lowered his head when he got to the curb where a couple of Alicia's neighbors were talking by their mailboxes. As soon as the coast was clear, he sat back up, then hit the steering wheel with his fist.

"This is bullshit!" he yelled.

Chapter Twelve

Bryce pulled the car over at a light to try and get his emotions under control as rain poured down on the windshield. Every time he went on a date something seemed to go wrong, so he wondered if agreeing with Seven's idea would play out in the end. *How could I let her put me in a situation where I almost got caught fucking a man's pregnant wife? What if that was me? I would lose my mind if I came home and found Seven fucking another dude. I would be under the jail because of some shit like that*, he thought staring out of the window. Bryce was so engulfed in his thoughts he didn't even hear when Jay-Z's *Dead Presidents* started to play. His ring tone was annoying to most, but Bryce was a big Jigga fan. When Bryce finally realized that he'd missed the call, he quickly called the number back.

"Hey, what's going on my nigga?" Bryce asked when Mitch answered.

"I was just checking on you. You haven't been calling me to take you to work," Mitch replied.

"Seven's been taking me lately, but I didn't go to work today. I had an errand to run."

"Oh really. Damn, you never take off. That must've been an important ass errand."

"Yeah, I guess you could say that."

"Well, why don't you meet me at Temptations so we can

have a drink? It sounds like you could use one," Mitch said.

"I'm tired. I need to get home," Bryce responded even though the first part was a lie. He wasn't tired, but he did want to get home. He had a serious bone to pick with his wife.

"You need to bring your ass down here. I haven't talked to you since you got kicked out the club." Mitch couldn't hold in the slight chuckle.

"I'm glad you find that shit funny," Bryce replied.

"I knew Seven had the skills to drive niggas crazy, but damn. She got your ass acting a fool."

If only you knew, Bryce thought.

"Come on man…one drink," Mitch pleaded.

"Okay, I'll meet you, but not at Temptations. Speedy is probably still pissed after the scene I caused. Let's go over to Player's Lounge."

"I'm already at Temptations since my shift starts in a few hours. Don't worry, Speedy isn't here. Plus, you should know we have better dancers to look at over here. Player's Lounge dancers look like crack-heads with stretch marks and bullet holes."

"What about the bouncers? I don't want any problems."

"Man, ain't nobody thinking about them punk ass niggas. Look, just stop by and have one drink, then you can leave. Shit, you know I'm paying," Mitch responded.

"What the hell you doing at the strip club in the middle of the day anyway? I didn't even know that place opened this early. Why aren't you at the construction site?"

"Haven't you looked outside? It's raining. You know we can't get much done when it's coming down like this. Besides, I'm pissed off anyway. They just hired a new Crane Operator, and I found out from the payroll girl that his ass makes ten thousand more than I do. And I'm supposed to be Lead Forman. Instead of them giving me that money, they gave it to a white muthafucka."

"That's fucked up."

"I know. I should quit," Mitch said.

"Well, you got the bartender job as a backup," Bryce responded.

"Yeah, but I need that construction income coming in too since my mom always needs my help."

"Stop faking. You need it for those hungry ass bitches you fuck with."

All Mitch could do was laugh.

"You know what…fuck it. I'm on my way to get that drink," Bryce replied. "Not only am I'm coming to get that drink, but it's my treat."

"Hello." Mitch tapped the phone. "I must be hearing shit. I thought you just said you were paying."

"You heard right. I got this one."

"Damn, did you hit the fucking lottery? I'm so used to you crying broke that I thought your ass would never pick up a check again."

Bryce wanted to tell Mitch about the new shit Seven had him doing, but quickly changed his mind. Mitch was the type of guy who would clown your ass until you were ready to fight. "I found a gig outside the garage that paid me as soon as the job was done."

"Oh, that's what's up. Okay, I'll see you when you get here then," Mitch said with excitement.

Bryce hung up the phone, then finally pulled off, making his way toward the club. With his head leaned against the seat, he was listening to Kem on the radio when his cell phone rang again. This time it was Seven, but Bryce refused to answer.

"All she wants to do is to grill me about that Alicia shit, and I'm not in the mood right now," Bryce said, putting his phone down in the passenger seat.

His phone ended up ringing three more times when he finally pulled into the parking lot. He knew Seven was gonna be pissed since he'd ignored all her phone calls, but for once Bryce didn't care.

When Bryce walked up to the door, the bouncer searched him, then checked his I.D. Luckily, it was a totally different guy from the other night.

"It's a two drink minimum," the bouncer said handing the license back.

After paying the cover charge, Bryce spotted Mitch sitting near the stage. As Lexi hypnotized Mitch with every move, he didn't even notice when Bryce sat down at the table. Bryce startled Mitch when he smacked him on the back.

"Where you come from dog?" Mitch asked.

Bryce laughed then ordered a Long Island Iced Tea from a passing waitress. "I see that Lexi hasn't lost her ability to mesmerize you."

"You know me," Mitch answered. "I love a big ass and a smile."

When the red light came on, Lexi picked up her money and blew Mitch a kiss. Mitch stood up and clapped as she walked down the steps toward the back room. His claps got louder as the waitress brought Bryce his drink and a refill on Mitch's Hennessey and Coke. Mitch's eyes widened when he saw Bryce peel off two twenty dollar bills from a huge stack of money and tossed it on the small serving tray.

"Twenty is for the drinks, and the other twenty is for you," Bryce informed the smiling waitress. It felt good to have money again.

"Damn, you weren't faking were you? That's a lot of dough you're rocking. How many jobs did you do today?" Mitch asked.

"Just one."

"That's what's up." Mitch sat down and held up his drink. "To bitches. You can't live with 'em, but who the fuck wants to live without 'em?"

"I second that," Bryce said raising his glass.

They were in the middle of their third drink when Rain came over to their table. Not even bothering to say hello, she pushed Bryce back and immediately started giving him a lap dance. Mitch looked over and smiled, but when Bryce quickly pushed her off of his lap, Mitch's smile faded.

"You don't want a lap dance, sexy?" Rain whispered into Bryce's ear.

"It's not that. I just came to get a drink, then head home to my loving wife." The last thing Bryce needed was for someone to go back and tell Seven a bunch of lies.

"Oh yeah, that's right. I forgot you have your own personal dancer at home. How's my girl doing anyway? I heard she's washing hair now," Rain said with a huge smirk. Realizing Bryce wasn't gonna bite, she stood up.

"Hell, I'll take that lap dance if he doesn't want it," Mitch chimed in.

"Mitch, you better fucking pay me for this," Rain fired back as she sat on his lap.

As Bryce enjoyed Rain's little performance, his cell phone started to ring.

"Nigga, you need to take that ring tone off," Mitch said.

"Don't hate on Jay, nigga," Bryce shot back.

After looking down at the number and seeing the name, 'Wifey' pop up, Bryce knew he couldn't answer once again. Seven would kill him if she found out where he was. Not to mention she was expecting him over an hour ago.

"I'm about to head out," Bryce said, downing his last drink.

"Thanks for stopping by and having a few drinks with your boy. Oh shit…and paying. It's been a while since we did this," Mitch replied.

Bryce pulled the knot of money back out, then dropped a few bills on Rain's breast. "This one is on me Mitch," he boasted.

Bryce gave Mitch a pat on his back, then headed outside. Bryce was a little tipsy so the drive home took a little longer than usual. It even took him a minute to get up to his door. When he finally entered the apartment, Seven wasn't eagerly waiting for him on the couch as usual. Instead, she was on the phone, pacing the living room floor. The tension radiated from her face as her heavy breathing sounded like she was experiencing an asthma attack. As soon as Bryce walked over to give her the money from Alicia's job, Seven slammed the phone down and snatched the money out of his hand.

"What do you have to say for yourself?" she shouted.

Oh shit, she's heard about me being at the club all ready. "What are you talking about?" he asked trying to play dumb.

"I just got off the phone with Alicia. She said your services were mediocre to say the least. So, like I said, what do you have to say for yourself?"

Bryce tilted his head. He felt like a child being scolded by his mother. "Are you really serious right now? The woman was pregnant. And I'm not talking a couple weeks pregnant. She was on the verge of delivering any day pregnant," Bryce responded. "Besides, if I was in there trying to knock her back out, I would've never heard her fucking husband pulling up. I can't believe you put my life in jeopardy. I could've been killed, but that shit doesn't seem to matter. You need to get your priorities straight."

"My priorities are straight. I don't give a damn if she was in the delivery room and the baby was crowning. You better not ever leave another woman unsatisfied. That was one of the rules, remember? How the hell are we gonna get future clients if the word gets out that you can't fuck?"

"Hold up. You need to pump your brakes," Bryce said.

"No. You're taking your ass right back over there and you're gonna fuck her pregnant ass until that bitch's vision gets blurry!" Seven yelled.

"You can't be serious. Her husband came home while I was there, Seven! Do you not understand? It's no way in hell I'm going back over there. I don't care what Alicia tells you or anybody else. My safety is way more important than this escorting bullshit. This whole situation is making you crazy."

"If you're not gonna take this shit serious, then just say so. I'll call and get my shift back at the club and we're done. What do you think about that?"

Bryce shook his head. "Think about what?"

"Think about me going back to work at the club. Since you were just there, I guess you won't mind." Bryce thought he'd gotten away with his midday outing, but obviously he hadn't. "You can't do too much without me knowing, and if you gave our money to any of those dirty hoes, it's gonna be a problem."

Seven stood there and counted the money, while beads of sweat began to pop up on Bryce's forehead. "Either that pregnant bitch is lying or you spent my money down at that fucking club because this shit is short. Alicia told me she gave you $900.00. It's only $700.00 in here!" she said in a stern voice.

"*Your* money? It's my money, too. I'm not your damn employee. If I wanna stop to have a drink with my boy, then that's what I'm gonna do," Bryce retorted. "I haven't been able to keep one dollar from these dates."

Seven frowned her face up. She then peeled off several twenties from the stack, then threw them in Bryce's direction. "You want your money. There it is…minus what you fucking spent."

"I don't care how many tantrums you have. I'm not going back over to that woman's house, so get that shit out of your head."

"All I know is that you better not leave another client unsatisfied or we're done," she warned.

Bryce couldn't believe how easy Seven was willing to walk away from their marriage. "You know I'm tired of you threatening me about this shit," he said before picking up the money.

"Oh really? Well, if you did what the fuck I told you, then you wouldn't have to be." Turning around, Seven walked to their bedroom and slammed the door.

Chapter Thirteen

Bryce was shocked to find Seven sitting on the couch watching *The Real Housewives of Atlanta* and eating chocolate covered peanuts when he got home. He was covered in grease from working on cars all day while she was obviously relaxing.

"What are you doing here?" he asked. "I thought Camille liked you to stay later on Wednesdays."

"I didn't feel like going anywhere today, so I called in sick," Seven replied without even looking up.

"So, you stayed home again. That makes two days in a row," Bryce said.

Seven finally looked up. "And…" Her communication had been brief and snappy since their fight a week before.

"Well, if you stayed home why didn't you think to come pick me up? I had to catch the bus again."

"What part of I didn't feel like going anywhere didn't you understand?" Seven snapped.

"So, you get to stay home while I bust my ass. That's real good," Bryce complained.

Seven rolled her eyes. "Ain't that how it's supposed to be?"

Bryce shook his head in disbelief. The fact that Seven would be lying around doing nothing and allow him to find his own way home was foul. But instead of getting into another heated argument, he decided to take a shower. He was dead tired from all the cars he'd worked on and the thought of having to do it again the next day made him even more drained.

He returned to the living room about thirty minutes later with Seven still in the same position as before. This time she was cracking up at the women fighting on the show. When he sat down, Bryce expected her to move away, but surprisingly she snuggled up next to him.

As soon as a commercial came on, Seven pulled out several pamphlets and passed them over to Bryce. He looked at the first one and grinned. They were advertisements for different types of classes including massage therapy, cooking, hand dancing and proper etiquette skills.

"Those little things will really enhance you for future dates. You'll be the total package," Seven said.

"How about I give you this total package right now?" Bryce said, pointing to his dick.

"I'm not in the mood. Maybe we'll try the sex thing in the morning."

"You're so damn moody. Sometimes you're ready to screw my brains out, while other times all you wanna talk about is business. For example, after our fight last week, you didn't say two words to me until you got a call inquiring about an escort date. From that point you got all giddy. You talked to me right up until I came back home with the money. After that, you went right back into your fucked up mood again."

"You better be glad Alicia even referred you to someone else after that stunt you pulled."

Bryce didn't respond as his mind traveled back to his last rendezvous. His date, Tammy, opened the door wearing only a robe. Since she was strictly paying for sex, Bryce didn't waste any time with small talk. He walked in and immediately began taking off his clothes. Tammy was a very powerful business woman in New Orleans who owned several McDonalds restaurants which later financed her acquisition of two hotels.

Tammy wasn't the most disgusting woman Bryce had done business with, but she was ugly enough that it took a little something extra for him to become aroused. Bryce didn't know why, but it wasn't Seven who entered his thoughts while he sexed Tammy. He did however have visions of Angelique.

"Business comes before feelings," Seven said, interrupting his thoughts.

"See, that's all you care about now."

"I'm sorry if you're feeling neglected in some way, but this *business* is gonna help us with our bills and then some," Seven responded.

"Speaking of bills, how many dates do you think I need to go on before I can get the down payment for the garage?"

"Oh, I see how you are. You don't mind talking about issues dealing with business and money when it concerns you," Seven snapped. "You should be able to get the down payment in time. Just let me handle the money. You just keeping looking good and working my dick and everything will be fine," she added.

"How much have you saved?" Bryce asked in a different tone.

"Well, I paid some bills, bought you a few items, signed you up for some classes, and bought two dresses for myself along with some shoes. I mean if I'm going to broker deals with women, I need to look a certain way, too. They won't take me serious in an outfit from Target. Hell, I need a new laptop because the one I have is ancient, but I'll wait on that," she rambled.

"So, basically we don't have any savings? Is that what you're saying?"

"We have a little bit. Not as much as we could have though. We can put what you made with Tammy toward savings though."

After their big Alicia blowout, Bryce ended up giving his half of the money right back to Seven to keep the peace and keep her happy, which didn't work out anyway.

"I need a new pair of steel toe boots for work. That's why I'm asking," Bryce stated.

"Well, you'll just have to make do with the ones you

have for now. We really do need to save."

Bryce gave Seven an, "are you serious" frown. Right before he opened his mouth to respond, the loud ring tone from Seven's phone interrupted him. Bryce watched as she pulled out a new, white I-phone from her purse. The line went dead just when she finally answered.

Bryce held a confused expression. "Whose phone is that?"

"It's my business phone. I couldn't keep walking around with that old ass Blackberry, so I upgraded it today. I have to be professional at all times."

"Hold up, so you can buy whatever you want, but I can't? Why the fuck didn't you add that phone to the shit you just listed?" Bryce roared. "And I thought you said you didn't feel like going anywhere today. You're just full of fucking lies, huh?"

Suddenly, her cell phone rang again. When Seven looked at the number, to her surprise it was Tammy. Their reactions were totally different. Seven wondered if Tammy was calling to complain about something that Bryce didn't do on their session. Bryce on the other hand was hoping that she didn't want a second date.

"Hello, Ms. Tammy," Seven answered.

"Hey girl, I was just calling to invite you and Bryce to my swinger Mardi Gras party at my house on Friday. I figured it would be a good place for you to meet some new clients and have a lot of fun, too," Tammy replied.

The thought of making new clients really got Seven excited. She looked over at Bryce and smiled. Bryce however shook his head as to say 'what the hell are you agreeing to now?' When Seven hung up and told Bryce about the upcoming party, his reaction was completely opposite from hers.

"I don't wanna go to no swinger party."

"Come on. We haven't been on our own date in a long time. This would be a good place to have some fun," Seven tried to convince.

"Seven, I've had enough of your lying for one day. You only wanna go to meet other women, and if that's the case I'll pass."

Seven sighed. "I'm staring at the man I love, but I can't help but wonder why does the bitch in him keep showing up? I don't get you. You whine about not being able to provide me with the things I deserve. You gripe because you have to fuck other women to pay off our debts and now you're complaining about having to take me to an orgy party that will further our business."

"You can taunt me all you want because I still don't wanna go," Bryce replied.

Seven was just about to plead her case, when her cell phone rung again. Looking at the screen, she became a little uneasy when the words, *Private* came across the screen. Relieved once the ringing stopped, her nervousness came right back when the phone rung yet again.

"Aren't you gonna answer that?" Bryce asked. "Maybe it's a *client*," he said in a condescending tone.

Seven shook her head. "No, it's just Camille. I don't feel like talking right now." She took the phone to the bedroom, before quickly coming back out. "Now, where were we? Oh yeah, this is where we were."

Seven fell down to her knees and grabbed Bryce by the waist. "Let me show you how sorry I am for being such a bitch." Pulling out his dick, Seven immediately went to work. It wasn't long before Bryce closed his eyes and started to moan.

It's like taking candy from a baby. As long as I can make him quiver, it will always be my way, Seven thought.

BEDROOM GANGSTA

Chapter Fourteen

"I'm about to blow your back out," Bryce whispered as he escorted a tall, brown skin woman into the guest bedroom at the end of the hall.

As the woman laid on the bed and removed her clothes, Bryce softly pecked her neck and shoulder. With her naked body fully exposed, he then started sucking both nipples while simultaneously rubbing his hands up and down her long, silky legs. It didn't take long for her pussy to become soaking wet. At that moment she grabbed his butt cheeks, motioning that she was ready to feel him inside of her. Realizing that was his signal, Bryce quickly obliged her by taking off his clothes, putting on a condom, and sliding his dick into her awaiting walls.

Bryce eased more of his swollen shaft inside her as the woman let out a seductive moan. Moments later, he began grinding his muscular frame in a circle, banging against her deepest erotic spots. Bryce didn't notice when the bedroom door opened and someone entered the room. He did however finally look up once he saw the silhouette walking toward him. It was Seven. Like a school administrator observing a tenured teacher, she sat down in a chair a few feet away from the bed and watched as Bryce gave the woman several deep thrusts.

How could she sit there and watch me do this, he thought.

"Oh my God, isn't that your boss sitting over there," the woman whispered when she realized that someone else was in the room.

Bryce hated Seven had to be referred to as that. But that sounded better than pimp.

"Yes, but don't worry. She doesn't mind."

Although he was extremely uncomfortable, Bryce knew he had to put in work in order to get this over with so he decided to kick things up a notch. He looked over at his beautiful wife before lifting up the woman's right leg high into the air giving him a good angle to ram his shaft even further.

Her body began to shake. "Your dick feels so good. Give me all you got baby," she said sticking her fingernails into his back.

Once his tool was dripping wet with her juices, he started to pound his dick until her moans turned into screams of ecstasy. Bryce smiled as her head jerked from side to side like the little girl from *The Exorcist* movie. The juicer her pussy got it seemed as if she was pissing on him with each stroke.

"Yes! Work the shit out of her, baby," Seven finally said.

Bryce glanced over at his wife watching his every move and nodded. Giving her a show, he sat up and placed both of the woman's legs onto his shoulders. Bryce then locked both of his hands onto her waist, then pulled her body so that his dick could knock against the back of her womb.

"You're incredible! Oh yes!" the woman screamed.

Bryce rolled her over keeping his dick inside until the woman's body was in the doggy style position. Grabbing her long hair, he pulled her backwards pounding areas of her pussy that she didn't even know existed. If that wasn't enough, Bryce extended his other hand and massaged her clit while still working her nest like a jack hammer on a busy highway.

"I'm about to explode!" she belted. "Oh my God."

"Okay honey, you can stop now. Her time is up. Besides, I need to go discuss some business with a few people who might want to meet you." Seven stood up and stretched.

"No…please don't stop. I was about to cum," the woman pleaded. She desperately wanted more.

"Bryce, did you hear me?" Seven's tone went from soft and timid to boisterous and commanding. "I said her time is up."

Not wanting to piss Seven off, he immediately stopped like a trained puppy. The woman's pussy farted as he quickly pulled out and scurried to get his belongings.

"Oh no. Please, just a little longer," the woman begged.

"Look, it's not my fault that you didn't reach your orgasm within your paid time limit. But he can keep it going if you have the money to pay his overtime fee. We charge a hundred dollars for every half hour," Seven said as she made the prices up.

"I don't have any more money on me. I didn't go to the ATM before I got here," the woman explained.

"Well, I'm sorry then. Nothing in this world is free, especially my escort's dick," Seven replied. The minute she gave Bryce a certain look, he rushed to put back on his clothes.

"Leave your shirt off. I want everybody to see what you're working with," Seven advised.

"I've never been fucked like that before in my life. You were so worth the money," the woman praised. "I mean the best."

"Thank…"

But before Bryce could finish, Seven cut him off, "Let's go. Don't say another word to her or you'll deal with me later." She looked over at the woman. "If he was the best, make sure you tell all your friends. Oh, and next time bring more money."

Seven grabbed Bryce by the arm and led him out of the bedroom to the area where everyone was hanging out. She blew kisses to friends and winks to sexy eye candy as they passed by. However, Seven's upbeat demeanor quickly faded as woman after woman made advancements toward Bryce, begging to be his next session.

"He's not free ladies. If you don't have money, keep it moving," she warned.

Even though she knew how irresistible Bryce was, Seven didn't want him to be with any of the broke looking women. She was on the prowl for clients with large bank accounts and not Burger King budgets.

When Seven walked past the kitchen, she did a double, then triple take at one of the women inside. It was one of Camille's clients from the salon.

"Deserae, is that you?" Seven said entering the room.

Deserae quickly turned around. "Oh, hey Seven. How are you?" She didn't seem the least bit embarrassed by being at a swinger's event as they gave each other a hug.

"Girl, I didn't know you rolled like this."

"Hell, I didn't know you rolled like this either," Deserae responded.

"I'm actually here on business," Seven tried to say in a professional tone.

"Oh yeah, I heard from Tammy that you were renting some guy out on personal dates. She also told me that he was excellent in bed. My good for nothing husband is out of town for the week, and I have my check book," Deserae said with a slick smile.

Luckily, Bryce had only been to the shop two times, so most people didn't know what he looked like.

Seven's face lit up. "If you really want him for a week I could give you a good price. Let's talk numbers, but it's cash only."

As Seven conducted business, Bryce walked over to the refrigerator to retrieve a couple of Jell-O shots. He quickly tossed them down, before reaching for a Heineken.

Seven looked around to see where Bryce was, so she could introduce him. "Where did he go?"

"Is that him over there drinking a beer?" Deserae pointed.

"Yeah. Bryce, get over here!" Seven shouted.

Knowing exactly what his wife was up to, Bryce lifted the frosted beer bottle up to his lips, then took a huge swallow.

When he decided to take another gulp, this time the beer started spilling. It ran down his smooth, chiseled jaw before dripping onto the large lion tattoo on his chest.

"Bryce, I'm waiting," Seven repeated with a different tone.

As Bryce walked over, Deserae's eyes were glued to his body wishing that he would ask her to lick him clean. Deserae was so hypnotized by Bryce that she didn't even realize when her tongue started tracing the exterior of her lips.

"Hey," Seven said, snapping her fingers in front of Deserae's face. "This is my escort's dick. Isn't it big?"

A large smile overcame Deserae's face. "What did you just say?"

"I said this is my escort, Bryce. Isn't he fine?"

Deserae smiled even harder realizing that she'd heard something totally different. "Hello, Bryce. Nice to meet you."

"Seven! I thought that was your fake ass!" a voice shouted from the other side of the kitchen.

All three of them looked over to see Hypnotic rushing in their direction. "I can't believe you!" she screamed.

"Who the fuck are you yelling at?" Seven responded.

"I'm yelling at you, bitch. I can't believe you stole my idea. I heard about you and your husband's little business. Is that why you called me that day wanting my cousin's number? I thought we were cool. How could you stab me in the back and run with my money maker?" Hypnotic was within inches of Seven's face.

"I know you better back the fuck up and change your tone. I'm not some dumb broad you can just come at like that," Seven replied as Deserae moved out of harm's way.

When Bryce tried to grab Seven's arm, she quickly snatched away.

"You're a simple bitch to think I'm gonna let you get away with stealing money out my pocket," Hypnotic warned.

"Oh, you throwing out threats now?"

"Damn right, you scandalous bitch."

"Well, in that case I'm about to turn this thing into a Fortune 500, and it ain't shit you can do about it!" Seven said pushing Hypnotic in the chest.

Hypnotic fell back against the wall. The crowd of people watching all backed up as she came back toward Seven with her hands swinging wildly. Seven dodged the first barrage of punches until one managed to land right above her lip. They clinched in an embrace and started scratching and punching each other until they both fell to the floor. With Seven landing on top, she grabbed Hypnotic by the hair and slammed her head against the floor.

Bryce ran over and snatched Seven away. "Let's go!" he yelled as Seven continued to swing. He managed to get her to the other side of the room before loosening his grip around her waist.

"We're not leaving. It's too much fucking money in this party to let a jealous bitch like that mess things up," Seven answered while she watched a couple of guys help Hypnotic into a chair.

Bryce shook his head in disbelief when he noticed the small bruise forming under Seven's nose. "Look at what this shit is doing. I knew this was a bad idea."

"Don't start that shit because of her. Come on so I can finish my conversation with Deserae," Seven said, pulling Bryce's arm.

"Bitch, this ain't over. You better believe me when I say this is a long way from being over!" Hypnotic wailed as the guys escorted her out of the kitchen.

"Fuck you!" Seven shot back.

Bryce let out a huge sigh. "I think we need to leave."

"No, I need to finish talking to Deserae and I also need to find Tammy. Do you think I can leave you alone for a while? I don't want you getting into any trouble."

"You're the one in here fighting like some hood rat, so you stay out of trouble. Hurry up and finish so we can roll out," Bryce said.

Giving him a quick peck, Seven quickly vanished into another room. Bryce spent the remainder of the night drinking and watching the party goers engage in all sorts of sexual episodes. As soon as he started to yawn, he knew it was time to leave. When Bryce went looking for Seven, he finally found her in the basement family room talking with three guys. Bryce knew she couldn't have been setting up any dates, so he wondered what she was doing.

"How much money are you talking about?" one of the guys asked.

Bryce walked up on the group with an instant attitude. "What the hell is going on?"

"Guys, this is the head liner for my escort business, Bryce" Seven introduced. Bryce could tell that she'd been drinking.

"He won't be once I start working," another man said with a laugh.

"What the fuck are they talking about?" Bryce questioned in a harsher tone.

"Honey, I was just thinking, we're making good money, but think about all the money we're missing out on because it's only you. Women are eventually gonna be turned away if you're booked, and I don't want that to happen. If we had more guys in the business, we could make even more money," Seven advised.

"Are you crazy? Now you wanna bring on more dudes. I thought this was gonna be something short term until we…" Bryce stopped himself before he told the whole world their business. "It seems like you're trying to make a career out of this shit."

"Why don't you go have another drink? We can discuss this later when we get home," Seven said.

"No, I'm ready to go. Especially now after seeing you trying to expand this shit into a fucking empire," Bryce responded.

"Bryce, don't embarrass me. I still have some clients to see and finish up with these guys. You have the keys. Why don't you take my car home and I'll get Tammy or one of the other girls to drop me off in a little while," Seven said.

Bryce was pissed. "I said, I'm ready to go!"

"The key word in that sentence was I'm…not we. If you're ready to go then leave. I still have work to do so I'm staying," Seven replied in a nasty tone. "Like I told you, I'm still conducting business, so just take my car. Just make sure you're home when I get there."

Little smirks were on each of the guy's faces as Bryce looked around the room. He was beyond embarrassed. He reached into his pocket and pulled out the keys to the car.

"Since you want to stay, here…I'll find my own way home," Bryce replied before throwing the keys in his wife's direction. He could feel all eyes on him as he turned around and stormed away.

"That was such a bitch move. Don't mind him though, he's had a lot to drink. He'll be behind this one hundred percent," Seven ensured the guys.

When Bryce made it to the front door, he turned around to see if Seven was following him. Realizing that she wasn't, he slammed the door behind him and power walked toward the end of the driveway. *The average wife would've tried to stop me*, he said to himself.

A pair of car lights blinded Bryce as he walked down the street to the entrance of the cul-de-sac. He lifted his hand to shield the lights, the closer the car approached.

"Hey Bryce, is that you?" a voice called out from the shadows.

He had no idea who the woman was. "Who's that?"

"It's me, Angelique," she said, turning off her headlights.

Immediately Bryce's persona changed. He no longer felt enraged at Seven for trying to acquire more men or knowing the fact that she hadn't saved any money. Once he realized it was Angelique, a smile displayed across his face. He walked closer to her car.

"Hey, what's going on? Hold up, I know you weren't

about to come to a swinger's party? I wouldn't think in a million years that a woman of your caliber would get down like that," Bryce said.

Angelique's eyes increased. "This is a what kind of party? I'm going to kill my damn cousin. She told me that this was just a little get together with some of her friends."

Bryce laughed. "You were about to get set up."

"Well, knowing what type of business you're in, I know why you're here," Angelique replied. "I'm so glad I ran into you. I wish you weren't leaving though."

"Yeah, I'm a little upset, so I need to get out of here. I should've never come in the first place. I just want to get home and try to be normal for a change."

"Normal sounds really good. With my work schedule I can't remember the last time I just had one of those types of days," Angelique agreed. "So, how are you planning to get there? Were you getting ready to walk home?"

Bryce nodded his head.

"Oh no, you don't have to walk. I'll take you home," Angelique offered.

Bryce looked back toward the house to see if any one was watching. "Are you sure?"

"Don't be silly. Of course."

Seven happened to be walking past one of the large bay windows when she saw Bryce getting into the passenger's side of the car. *Who the fuck is driving that Benz? Bryce doesn't know any body rolling like that. He better not be taking a client without me setting it up and getting my fucking money.*

Chapter **Fifteen**

Bryce slid his body into Angelique's car and slammed the door.

"I know you're upset but that's no reason to take it out on my car," Angelique said.

"I'm sorry. I have a lot on my mind. Please excuse me," Bryce responded.

Angelique laughed while slowly turning her Benz around. When she looked over at Bryce it really did seem like he had the weight of the world on his shoulders. "Are you sure you're good with this? I don't want to cause any problems."

"No, I'm straight."

"Good. Do we wanna stop by a bar and get a shot or two to calm you down before you go home? Do you have time?"

When Bryce thought about Seven pissing him off back at the swinger's party, he could care less about getting to the house by a certain time. "Yeah, as a matter of fact, I could use a drink."

Angelique smiled. "Great," she said, before making a right on Stanton Road, and headed straight for Bourbon Street.

Normally, Angelique didn't like hanging in the French Quarter since it was always congested with tourists. But knowing the bars made the best Hurricanes, she made an exception. After driving a few more minutes, Angelique parked on a side street, then led the way to the first bar she could find. Bryce couldn't take his eyes off the way her ass jiggled in the black, one shoulder Alice & Olivia Dress. Even the Gucci Akerman open-toe booties made her calves look like mini oranges. She was the epitome of a runway model.

Walking into Razzoo's, they slid into an orange booth lined against the wall before Angelique ordered a Bacardi Hurricane for herself and two shots of Hennessey for Bryce. As soon as the waitress left, he rested his head against the cushioned pad.

"I'm losing control of all of this," Bryce spoke over the live band.

"What do you mean?"

He shook his head. "Seven is taking this escort thing way too far. I believe at the end of the day, it won't be that pot of gold that we hoped for," he said, reaching for his shot as the waitress returned.

"Nothing is ever what it seems and it's a fact that no matter how much we plan, the likelihood of things ending up in that order is unlikely," Angelique responded.

"Do you know she actually had the nerve to try and recruit more guys at the swinger's party?" Bryce said tossing his first shot back.

"She sounds like a savvy business woman to me. The more guys she has leads to more money, right?"

"So, I guess you think I'm overreacting to the whole idea, huh?"

Seven sipped her drink. "Actually, I do. What difference does it make how many guys she brings on? What…you want all the money to yourself or something?"

Bryce wanted to tell Angelique about Seven being his wife, but something told him it wasn't a good idea. "It's more to it than that, but forget I even said anything. Let's talk about something else," Bryce said tossing another shot down.

Angelique and Bryce continued to talk until the conversations turned from complete sentences to broken fragments and loud laughter at things neither one of them found funny. Every now and then, Bryce paused to admire how sexy Angelique looked. It was the first time he noticed the way a little dimple appeared on the side of her mouth when she laughed.

"I don't think I can make it home by myself," Angelique said, trying to stand to her feet. She'd downed four Hurricanes.

Bryce laughed as she fell into his arms. "I guess I'll have to take you home then. Give me your car keys, Ms. Drunkie." They both laughed.

After paying for the bill with her Amex Black card, Bryce held Angelique steady so she could sign the receipt. Stumbling to the car, he pressed the unlock button on her key until her car lights blinked. When Bryce went to open the passenger's side door, he'd only let go of Angelique for a second before she fell down to the hard concrete. Bryce laughed as he helped her into the car.

"Damn girl, you really are wasted," he said, staggering around to the driver's side. He was drunk too, but no where near like Angelique. When they pulled off, Bryce made sure to drive extra careful, so he wouldn't get pulled over. On top of all his other problems, the last thing he needed was a DUI.

Bryce worked hard to keep Angelique from tipping over onto her hardwood floor when they walked into her condo. When he finally helped her over to the couch, he turned around to go get her some water, but Angelique obviously had another idea in mind. She stared into Bryce's eyes just before yanking his shirt open sending the buttons in every direction. Seconds later, they were both pulling at each other's clothing as their tongues fought one another violently. Angelique's soft skin felt better than he remembered. Bryce yanked on her bra snaps until they broke and her firm breasts were exposed.

Suddenly, Bryce pushed Angelique off of him as his head started to spin. At that point, he wasn't sure if it was the drinks or thoughts of Seven that began to dance around in his head.

I can't go through with this. I promised Seven that I would never kiss another woman or have sex with one without her knowing, Bryce thought to himself. *How many of her rules am I going to break?* He felt extremely guilty.

"Take me now Bryce, I want to feel you," Angelique moaned.

Bryce wondered what Seven was doing since she hadn't even bothered to call. He tried to picture her still talking to those guys with hopes it would justify his desire to take Angelique in his arms and fuck the shit out of her.

"I want you. Take all of me, Bryce," Angelique moaned again.

He couldn't resist her pleas any longer. Once he pulled off his pants, Bryce pulled Angelique down to the floor then removed her black thong in a forceful nature. They hadn't even had sex yet, and the moment was already different from their first encounter.

Bryce gently rubbed the side of Angelique's face as he inserted his penis into her wanting pussy. Her angel soft moans eased all the confusing tug-a-war games with Seven that had been weighing on his heart. Their breathing intensified as they kissed. Moments later, Bryce decided to change locations. He stood up and gathered Angelique off the floor and into his arms. Carrying her like an excited groom, Bryce quickly whisked Angelique into her bedroom and onto the plush leather upholstered bed.

She layed back on the bed with her legs wide open. "I'm ready to feel good, baby."

With a rock hard dick, Bryce crawled onto the bed and inserted it into her nest. It was soaking wet, which made him want to cum immediately. He tenderly rubbed her ass while going deeper into her vagina until the tingling sensation made his toes curl.

With the urge to take charge, suddenly Angelique rolled Bryce over onto his back and sat down on his shaft. She pressed her nails into his chest lowering her body until his entire dick was devoured by her pulsating pussy. Moments later she started moving her body up and down at a rapid pace. Bryce grabbed her thighs to hold her still as her clit vibrated on the tip of his dick.

"Hold it there and grind. You feel so good," Bryce called out.

"It feels so good!" Angelique yelled as the headboard began to bang against the wall. "I don't wanna stop…I'm cumming!"

That's all Bryce needed to hear as his own amazing orgasm rushed up his penis. "Shitttt…I'm cumming too baby!"

Bryce and Angelique locked hands until both of their orgasms ran their course. They held onto each other as the wonderful feelings took control of their bodies. Once they were done, Angelique snuggled up in Bryce's strong embrace for several minutes.

"Seven is my wife," Bryce blurted out.

Angelique shot back up and looked at him for several seconds. It was if the comment instantly made her sober. "Huh?"

"I said Seven is my wife." For some reason, Bryce felt the need to get everything out.

"Seven is your wife," Angelique replied in disbelief.

"Yeah. I lied to you before when I said she was just a friend."

"So, doesn't it bother her that you're having sex with other women?"

Bryce shook his head. "Obviously not, because this escort thing was her idea."

It seemed like Angelique was trying to process everything. "So, is she gonna be mad that you're here with me now? I mean, this wasn't planned like the last time."

"Probably so. But after the way she's been acting, I don't think I'm gonna tell her yet."

"Do you feel guilty now since we slept together without her knowing?"

It took Bryce a while to answer. "Yeah, I guess." What he really felt bad about was not wearing a condom.

"Wow, this is crazy. So, how does it feel having your wife as your pimp?" Angelique curiously asked.

"This is all new for me," Bryce replied even though he hated that word. "I was extremely hesitant at first, but when you're backed into a corner, you do things that go against everything you believe in."

"I can understand that. Looking back I made some professional moves that I probably wouldn't have if I didn't know it would get me closer to my goals. Still, I'm not sure if there's enough money in the world that would make me jeopardize my relationship if I was married to you. I would never share you with any other woman. No one deserves to feel you other than your wife."

Bryce was beyond flattered.

"Not to mention, your wife is only charging five hundred dollars for your sex services. Trust me when I say that's not even close to what you're worth," Angelique continued.

"Thanks, I appreciate that."

Angelique stared at Bryce before gently kissing him on his lips. "Your wife needs to appreciate you."

As if the timing was perfectly planned, they could hear Bryce's loud Jay-Z ring tone going off from the living room. When the ringing stopped, then started back up they both knew it was probably Seven.

"Are you gonna get that?" Angelique asked.

Bryce paused for a moment. "No, I'm not."

Chapter Sixteen

Seven was pissed when she pulled up to their apartment. She'd been calling Bryce nonstop for the past hour, and he still hadn't answered the phone. "He better be in the fucking house," she said as soon as thoughts of him getting into the Benz popped back up. Not knowing who the mysterious car belonged to; Seven could only hope that her husband had done the right thing by not going on a date.

"Even though it wasn't the same kind, Hypnotic is the only bitch I know rolling in a Benz right now. But then again, he would know better than that," Seven said, giving Bryce the benefit of the doubt. She glanced at the time on her radio. It was going on one a.m. "This muthafucka knows that I shouldn't be walking in the house by myself at this time of night."

After finding a parking space across the street from the building, Seven jumped out then hurried up the stairs. Knowing how crazy and unpredictable their neighborhood was, she couldn't put her key in the door fast enough. As soon as Seven turned the knob, she instantly started calling out his name.

"Bryce!" she yelled.

When he didn't answer, she ran into the bedroom turning on all the lights. Seven scratched her head trying to figure out why she was standing in an empty apartment. "Where the hell is he?"

Suddenly, Seven remembered Bryce's face when he left the swinger's party. *I know he was into his feelings, but now he's taking this shit too far*, she thought to herself.

Even though Seven knew she could've defused the situation by leaving with her husband instead of staying with several strange men, admitting to any wrong doing wasn't her best quality.

Seven pulled out her cell phone and dialed Bryce's number, but again it went straight to voice mail. After going into the kitchen to pour herself a glass of wine, she repeated the process of dialing his number a few more times before texting him to call her immediately. Seven tried to take her mind off of Bryce not responding by taking a quick shower and putting on her white wife beater and boy shorts, but it only made her angrier when she saw the time getting later and later. Each time Bryce's unenthused prerecorded message came on, the more pissed off she got.

Moments later, a soft tap on Seven's door caught her attention. Seven rubbed her hands across her face. She quickly tried to clean the apartment up by putting several items in their proper place before walking over to the door. Looking through the peephole, Seven released a huge sigh, then opened the door to let her next client Stephanie inside. She was holding a stack of crisp twenty-dollar bills.

"I'm here and ready to party!" Stephanie shouted.

"Girl, my neighbors are sleep. Get in here before you wake everybody up," Seven said ushering her inside.

"Where's my date? You promised me a night I would never forget. Let's get this thing going. Momma started her fire on the way over here and now I need a good hard fuck to finish the journey," Stephanie said falling onto the couch.

"Well…umm, he's still not home."

Stephanie's face quickly frowned. "He's not home? So, are you telling me that I drove all the way over here for nothing? What the fuck kind of business are you running?"

"He's never done this before. I never would've asked

you to come over if I had bad intentions. I don't play with people's sexual needs," Seven answered.

"This is the total opposite of what I thought you meant by *the night I'll never forget*," Stephanie said standing up.

"Please…sit down. I'll be right back," Seven said walking toward the bedroom.

I'm going to kill that no good nigga. He's fucking with my money now. He better have a damn good excuse for putting me in this unnecessary predicament, Seven thought as she hurried into the bedroom and removed what little clothes she had on. She grabbed a black leather strap-on from out of her nightstand drawer, then quickly searched through her dildos until she found one that compared to Bryce's dick. Putting everything on in record time, Seven rushed back out to the living room before Stephanie tried to leave.

Stephanie looked surprised when she saw Seven standing in the hallway with the strap-on hanging between her legs. "I promised you a night you'll never forget and that's what you're about to experience," Seven informed.

Stephanie became even more shocked as Seven pulled out a bottle of KY Touch Massage oil and started rubbing it all over the enormous dark chocolate synthetic penis like it really was connected to her body. Seeing how seductively Seven moved her hand, a large smile suddenly displayed on Stephanie's face. Stephanie stood up and licked her lips.

"Bend that ass over the chair and pull up that fucking skirt," Seven commanded.

Stephanie giggled in a joyous way while rushing to assume the position. Seven slowly walked over and yanked off the lace thong Stephanie had on.

"I don't know if you've ever been fucked by a woman, but what I'm about to do to you will never be duplicated," Seven bragged.

The late September sky appeared to be a large canvas of mixing colors as the sun began to rise from behind several clouds. It was almost 5:50 a.m. and Bryce was just tip-toeing into the apartment. He moved about with the sounds of a shadow making sure not to wake Seven, who he heard snoring in the bedroom. As he softly made his way around, every now and then he would pause to let the massive headache he had settle down. He hoped by the time she got up he would have the story of his whereabouts in tact. When Bryce went into the bathroom to grab a few Advils from the medicine cabinet, several items fell out onto the floor as soon as he opened the door. Being a complete rookie at staying out all night it seemed as if the quieter he tried to be, the more noise he actually made.

"Shit," Bryce said, bending down to pick everything up. By the time he stood back up, Seven was standing in the doorway with both hands on her hips. She stared at him with eyes that could cut steel.

"Where the fuck have you been? Do you know what time it is?" Seven yelled.

Bryce held up the Advil bottle. "Can I at least take one of these before you start?"

In a complete rage, Seven grabbed Bryce's cologne off the counter and threw it at his head. Luckily, he managed to duck as the glass bottle landed against the wall and shattered.

"Where the fuck have you been?" Seven repeated with a piercing pitch.

Bryce had planned to be nice until she decided to get violent. "I think you've forgotten that I'ma grown ass man." He tried to walk around her, but she just blocked his path.

"I saw you getting into that Benz outside the party. Whose car was that? I know it wasn't a dude. Don't play with me, Bryce. I know more than you think."

"Well, if that's the case, then you know who it was. If you're going to act like a detective and follow me around, then do your damn job," Bryce fired back.

"Have you've lost your fucking mind? The next words out your mouth better be the name of that bitch you rolled out with."

"I'm your husband, not your child. I'm not gonna stand here and let you talk to me like that." Bryce used his arm to move Seven out of the way, then walked toward their bedroom.

Seven stormed right after him. "Get your ass back here and tell me where you were all night. Do you know what I had to do because you weren't home?"

"Oh, let me guess, you had to actually park the car and open the door all by yourself. Damn, did you break a nail?" Bryce sarcastically replied.

Seven couldn't believe his attitude. She'd never seen him this cocky before. "This isn't a fucking joke. You damn near cost me some money!"

Bryce's expression showed that he could give a fuck less. "Oh really."

"Speaking of money, I need you to break me off with my cash. I know that so-called good samaritan in the Benz didn't get a free night with your broke ass in exchange for a ride home," Seven said, holding out her hand.

"Since you wanna take cheap shots, see how long it takes me to give you any answers."

Seven's eyes tightened. "You're so lucky."

"How do you figure that?"

"Because if Stephon was here when you finally decided to show up it would've been problems. I had to call him last night because I was scared to stay alone. He was pissed that you left me here by myself. You better be glad he had to make a run early this morning."

"Seven, don't threaten me with your drug dealing brother. If he comes and fucks with me, I know how to get rid of his ass. Besides, you've never been scared to stay by yourself."

"Well, I was this time. I can't believe you're walking in here with the sun, and got the nerve to have a fucked up attitude. Who does that?" Seven threw up her hands. "If it wasn't for my quick minded business sense you would've cost us a lot of money and future references with that little disappearing act. I had a client come home after the swinger party and you weren't even here. Do you know how embarrassing that was?"

Bryce looked at her with a blank stare. "You brought a client here? Now, I know you've lost your damn mind."

Seven decided to change her tone a bit to see if Bryce would soften as well. She knew once he was in that state, he'd be more willing to admit where he was. "You're my husband. The man who promised to fulfill all my needs once we were married. And now that I'm asking you to make good on those promises you wanna turn this around on me."

"I'm doing my fucking part, but it's obviously not good enough. Now, you've crossed the line by bringing some client to our house just to make a few dollars. I'm not turning anything around on you. I just think things are getting out of hand," Bryce replied. "Every since I agreed to do this, you've changed. I bet you're only asking about my whereabouts because you're worried that I fucked someone without charging."

"Well, did you?"

Bryce didn't respond.

"Don't hold your tongue now. You've been talking all big and bad up to this point. Why don't you finish off by telling me where you were?" Seven walked up to Bryce and shoved him in his chest.

"You need to calm the fuck down. I swear you're getting ready to cross a line that will not only cause you to lose so your called business, but your husband, too," Bryce warned.

"It would be like you to run out on me now with our business about to jump off and me being pregnant," Seven said as a single tear raced down her face.

Chapter **Seventeen**

"You're what?"

Seven sobbed even louder. "I'm pregnant. The reason why I've been acting so crazy is because my hormones are raging out of control. I took three of those home pregnancy tests just to confirm my suspicions, and all three came up positive. You're going to be a father."

When Bryce felt his knees buckle, he immediately sat down on the edge of the bed. He rubbed his hand over his face not knowing how to respond. He felt upset, confused, overwhelmed, and elated all at the same time. After being completely quiet for several minutes, he stood back up and pulled his wife toward him.

I got this nigga right where I need him now, Seven thought.

"How long have you known?"

"Umm, I took the test a couple of days ago. When it turned positive, I had no idea what to do. This is a real crazy time for us and a baby is definitely gonna make it even more hectic," Seven said, playing with his goatee.

"This is a hell of a way for you to tell me," he responded.

"I'm sorry, but the time never seemed right."

Bryce looked up at Seven. He felt so bad for his actions. "I'm sorry I stayed out last night. I was upset because it seemed like I was losing you to money and had no idea that it was your body playing tricks with your emotions. It's nothing to really tell you. I spent the night over Mitch's house," Bryce lied. He didn't want to tell Seven the truth and stress her out any further.

"So, what happened to your shirt?" Seven pointed to all the missing buttons.

Bryce swallowed the lump in his throat. Any sign of nervousness was a dead giveaway. He cursed himself for being stupid enough to walk around in the evidence. "Man, me and Mitch went to the French Quarter last night and got drunk as shit. You know how we fuck with each other all the time, so that big muthafucka ended up pulling on my shirt when we were pretending to fight." At least the first part was true.

"Who picked you up in the Benz last night?" Seven's interrogation was slightly intimidating.

"Actually you were dead set on it being a woman, but it was actually Mitch. When he came to pick me up, his ass was flossing in the car like the shit belonged to him." *Damn, I hope this sounds believable*, he thought.

"I think you're lying," Seven spoke in a stern voice.

Now, Bryce really thought shit was about to hit the fan. "Why would you say that?"

"Because I've never known for Mitch to fuck with a girl who had money. I mean, is he slinging dick that good?"

"Umm…I definitely wouldn't know about that."

Seven softened a bit. "You could've at least called. I was worried to death."

"I was pissed, even though I know that's not a good excuse." Bryce started rubbing Seven's stomach, then looked up and smiled. "You look hungry. Why don't you lay down and I'll fix you something to eat? You shouldn't be on your feet."

She chuckled. "I'm not hungry, baby. The gesture is so sweet, but trust me, I'm fine."

"What do you need me to do?" Bryce asked.

"All I need for you to do is to get out there on the dates I've lined up and make that money."

Bryce's face quickly turned upside down. "I know you don't wanna continue with this escorting thing with you being pregnant."

"How else are we gonna make it with another mouth to feed?"

"The garage will be more than enough to care for our family when I buy it."

Seven began laughing uncontrollably. "Are you serious? What you make escorting triples the amount of money that fucking garage will earn in a year. Besides, how are you gonna get the money to buy it if you don't escort?"

"That garage is good honest work that'll pay out in the end," Bryce said getting upset.

"I'm sorry baby. I didn't mean to upset you. I have total faith in you," Seven replied putting her arms around him. "I just was reminding you that buying the garage will take money and the only way I see us getting it is if you do a few more dates."

Suddenly, Angelique's face appeared in Bryce's thoughts. The guilt of him fucking her all night made his feelings toward Seven's plan fade. "I'm doing this only to get the money for the garage and after that it's done."

"That's why I love you so much." Seven kissed his forehead, then ran over to the nightstand.

"I need to spend more time at the garage so Darrell will know that I'm serious about buying it and not look for any other buyers. You have to keep that in mind as you set up these dates. I've missed a few days of work already so I can't miss too many more," Bryce informed.

"No problem," she said, retrieving an envelope from the drawer, then handing it to him. Bryce opened the envelope to find an airline confirmation to New York. "What's this?"

"I told you that we are on the brink of having this escorting thing take off. A client heard about our services all the way in NYC and wants to hire you for the weekend."

Bryce was actually shocked himself. "Who's the client?"

"I set this up a few days ago, but wasn't sure how I felt

about the date being out of town. Her name is Chase. She's a music exec at Sony. You'll be crossing the color line with her because she's white, but she's loaded."

Bryce closed his eyes. He thought about the idea of him having sex with a white woman. It had always been a fantasy of his that he never got to fulfill. A small grin appeared on his lips. "Remember, I'm only doing this for us and the baby," Bryce answered with a small lie included.

Seven kissed Bryce on the lips. "Pack a suit. Your plane leaves at twelve-thirty this afternoon."

Bryce looked back down at the paper. "When do I come back?"

"It should be a return confirmation in there for late Sunday evening around eight o'clock."

"Why am I staying so long?"

"Because that's what the client wanted. As long as she's paying for two days of service, who cares?"

Bryce didn't want to argue. "Cool. Well, let me take a shower and try to take a quick nap before I have to roll out," he said. "I'm beat."

As Seven walked out of the bedroom door, she leaned against the wall with a devilish smirk on her face. *Everything is working out just like I planned. I'm gonna get so much done with his ass out of town*, she thought.

"Good afternoon, Ms. Lyles," Angelique's secretary said as she walked into the office.
Angelique was supposed to be there hours ago, but it was almost twelve-thirty.

"Good afternoon, Regina. I had one of those nights. Can you bring me a few aspirins?"

"Sure, Ms. Lyles," Regina answered.

"Are there any messages for me?"

"No, but Christian Dwight, is already waiting in the conference room. He's been here about twenty minutes."

"Good, let him wait. Since he missed our first meeting and didn't bother to call, I need him to understand that we all have jobs to do. I bet if I'd missed a deal that cost him money he wouldn't tolerate that type of unprofessionalism on my part." Angelique was pissed that she had to be in the office on a Saturday, but it was the only day Christian seemed to be available. Angelique knew it wasn't right to keep a potential client waiting, but as severe as her headache was, she could care less.

As soon as Angelique went into her office, she immediately felt Bryce's hands rubbing up and down her body as she sat down in her leather chair.

"Why are all the good men married to the wrong women?" she pondered. "It never fails... the things in life that bring you the most pleasure are always the things you can't have."

When Angelique's office door opened moments later, Regina walked in with two aspirins and a bottle of Deer Park. "I like the way that outfit is fitting you," Angelique said.

A smile quickly appeared on Regina's face. She'd been working hard to try and get a handle on her weight. After her last pregnancy, she seemed to go up from a size eight to a size sixteen. "Thank you, Ms. Lyles. I'm doing that Zumba dance every night. I'm down to a twelve now, but my goal is to get to a ten before the month is out." Regina tugged on her pants.

"Keep it up. You're going to be so small, they'll have to send out a search party to find you."

Angelique quickly took the two pain relievers before strolling out of her office. She paused outside the glass conference room doors. *He really isn't bad looking for a white boy*, she thought looking at the rookie sensation from the Atlanta Thrashers hockey team.

When Angelique walked into the conference room, she sat a few files on the long rectangular cherry oak table, then sat across from Christian.

"Hello, Mr. Dwight. I'm sorry for my tardiness," Angelique said extending her hand.

"Yeah, I've been here for a while," Christian replied shaking her hand firmly. "I don't like wasting my time."

Angelique bit her tongue. She wasn't in the mood for another conceited, overpaid athlete, but if she wanted to make partner, unfortunately this is what she had to endure.

"That's understandable. Now, what is it that our firm can do for you?"

"Well, I've been told that you're the right person to work out my contract with the Thrashers. It's widely known that you work out the best deals between players and management," Christian replied.

"I guess we both did our homework. I researched your last contract and followed your stats over the year and I'm certain I can get you a stronger agreement."

"That's what I was hoping for. Let's get down to some specifics," Christian said shaking his head.

Angelique and Christian talked about his deal over the next hour and a half. She did a background analysis to figure out Christian's likes and future goals. The money part would be simple because of the salary caps, but getting all the endorsement deals would be the tricky part. The right signing was the difference between six and seven figures.

When they finished their meeting, Christian seemed pleased with the end results. Angelique had put together a very detailed plan that touched on all the things Christian hoped for and a few things he didn't.

"They said you were the best, and I'm glad to see that all the rumors were correct," he praised.

"And who are they?" Angelique asked closing her folders.

"My trainer works with a lot of ball players. When I talked to some of them about who should represent me, this firm and your name always found its way into the conversation," Christian said.

"Wait…you can't go in there!" Angelique heard Regina shouting as the conference door flew open.

Angelique and Christian both looked up to see Hypnotic walking into the room ignoring Regina's cries. Regina chased after her.

"I'm sorry, Ms. Lyles. I tried to stop her," Regina said. "Should I call security?"

"That won't be necessary. I'll handle it," Angelique answered.

Hypnotic waved her hand goodbye as Regina walked out of the office. Regina rolled her eyes just before closing the two glass doors as Hypnotic laughed it off. She walked over to hug Angelique.

"Umm…I'm in a meeting," Angelique said.

"Oh my, who's this sexy cup of milk?" Hypnotic said, ignoring her cousin.

Angelique was slightly embarrassed. "Christian, please forgive her. As you see, she's not one to be coy."

Christian's eyes followed Hypnotic's hour glass frame, starting at her five inch YSL pumps. Hypnotic's tight fitting Hudson skinny leg jeans exposed her firm butt cheeks as she walked over toward the conference table. Christian smiled when he noticed a silver chain connected to her belly ring that disappeared under her cropped t-shirt. He licked his lips knowing it was probably fastened to her nipple.

"What are we doing in here?" Hypnotic asked sitting on the table.

Angelique shook her head. "We were just finishing a deal."

Hypnotic turned to stare at Christian. "You're a sexy white boy. Are you some kind of baller? Let me guess, you play soccer or baseball."

"So, I look like a soccer or baseball player, huh?" Christian asked with a laugh.

Hypnotic slowly slid her tongue across her fire engine red lipstick. "As fine as you are, you could be a model. As soon as I walked in here, I wanted to masturbate instantly."

Christian's eyes widened. So did Angelique's.

"Umm Crystal, why don't you meet me in my office?" Angelique suggested. She wasn't about to say her stripper name in front of a client.

"I actually play hockey. Are you a fan?" Christian asked. He was ignoring Angelique as well.

"I'll be whatever you want me to be," Hypnotic shot back.

Angelique quickly jumped in before Christian could respond. "Okay, I think we're done. Let me walk you out Christian before this gets really inappropriate."

Christian and Hypnotic continued to stare at each other as he stood and shook Angelique's hand, then Christian walked over and held out his hand for Hypnotic.

"It was a pleasure meeting you. I hope to see you again," Christian said as he kissed the back of her hand.

"Angelique has all your information. If I want you, I know how to find you," Hypnotic answered.

Christian chuckled at her response. He glanced back a couple more times before he exited the conference room. Hypnotic quickly got off the table once the outer door closed.

"Are you crazy? Don't ever do that again. That shit could've easily gone the wrong way," Angelique said when she returned a few minutes later. "I know you like coming onto men, but these are my clients, not yours."

"Oh, Cuz, lighten up. I was just having fun."

"Well, I don't work for myself like you do, so have fun somewhere else." She motioned for Hypnotic to follow her back to her office. "How did you know he was paid anyway? He could've easily been the janitor."

"Girl, please, I can smell money a mile away," Hypnotic replied as they walked past Regina and into Angelique's office.

"You can go home now Regina. Thanks for coming in on a weekend," Angelique said just before closing the door.

Hypnotic took a seat. "I can't believe I had to come to

your job on a Saturday just to catch up with your ass. You haven't even been returning my phone calls."

Angelique strolled over to her desk. "I know. I've been so busy with work lately. So, what do you want to talk about? When you called me this morning you didn't even wanna wait until I got off, so it must be important."

"It's that bitch, Seven. When you told me that she called you to pitch her new escorting business, I've been trying to catch up with her ass ever since. The fact that she had the nerve to call you instead of trying to find her own clientele is pathetic, especially since she stole my idea!" Hypnotic yelled. "I saw her at that swinger's party you stood me up at last night, and we got into it. Muthafuckas had to end up taking me outside because it got so bad. I wanna kill that bitch!" Hypnotic banged her fist against the seat cushion.

"So…wait. She hit you? Is that why it looks like you have a black eye?"

"Yeah. I was wondering when you were gonna say something."

Angelique was pissed. Even though she was beginning to like Bryce, there was no way Seven was gonna get away with hitting her cousin. Where she was from, family always came first.

"Did you know that the guy she's pimping is her husband?"

Hypnotic's mouth flew open. "What? Hell no. I mean you only told me brief details about the date, like the fact that he could fuck real good, but since you never mentioned his name, I had no idea. I even saw him at the party, but still didn't think he was the escort. I just thought they were into kinky shit as a couple. Damn, did you know this prior to that date?"

"No, I just found out myself."

"That bitch is beyond scandalous. She must not have any feelings for her husband to do some shit like that."

Angelique nodded her head. "That's the same shit I said. How do you know her again?"

"We used to strip together. Then we started working for the same escort service until she quit. I was telling her about my male escort idea the day you came into Camille's salon. Now, look. I really need to figure out a way to get her ass back because she fucking played me."

"You know I got you, but I'm too old to be jumping girls like we did when we were teenagers. We have to be a little more clever and put together something that'll make a lasting mark. A simple beat down isn't enough."

"Well, I've been thinking. I can't come up with nothing besides running her ass over in the street with my car then backing that shit up three or four times."

Angelique laughed. "That's why I love you."

"If that nigga Bryce can fuck like you said, that escort business wouldn't be shit without him!" Hypnotic shouted.

It was if a lightning bolt hit Angelique. She stood straight up. "That's it."

"What's it?"

"You just said it. We'll get her back by doing something that she'll never be able to forget."

"The suspense is killing me. What are you thinking?"

"We're going to steal her most prized possession. We're going to take her husband," Angelique advised.

"Hell yeah, I love it. That shit would push her ass over the deep end," Hypnotic said with a huge grin. However moments later, her joyous expression disappeared. "Hold up…how are we gonna take him? Do you think it's gonna be that easy?"

This time Angelique smiled. "For the record, the reason why I stood you up last night is because I met Bryce outside the party. And to make a long story short, we fucked again. This time without her knowing, so yeah I think it's gonna be that easy."

Hypnotic couldn't seem to control her excitement. "Are you serious? Damn, I wish I could call Seven and rub it in her face right now."

Angelique shook her head. "That wouldn't be good

enough. Trust me, if we do it my way the sting will last a lot longer."

"That bitch has no idea what's coming," Hypnotic said.

BEDROOM GANGSTA

Chapter Eighteen

Bryce was so happy to be back home from the noisy streets of New York as he hailed a taxi from the airport's arrival area. After telling the driver his address, he slid down in the back seat and instantly closed his eyes. Tired and worn out, he was completely sleep deprived from being up so long. As soon as he arrived in New York the day before, Bryce checked into his hotel, then immediately met up with Chase to escort her to a charity event at Radio City Music Hall. From there they went to dinner, then back to his hotel room where the two of them fucked all night long.

Bryce laughed, making the taxi driver look in the rear view mirror to see what was going on. He shook his head when thoughts of Chase telling him, "Fuck me Mandingo," entered his mind. Bryce's sexual experience with a Caucasian had satisfied his curiosity, but did nothing to change his views on loving women of color. Especially when Chase constantly wanted him to smack her flat, ironing board ass. He also wasn't a fan of her fake boobs that she kept bragging about. He was thrilled when Chase got an urgent call from her mother at four a.m. regarding her father's health cutting his weekend date short. Spending another day with someone he had nothing in common with would've been nerve-racking.

Bryce didn't bother calling Seven to tell her that he was

on his way to the airport to wait stand-by for the first available flight home. He wanted to surprise his wife by sliding into bed and making love to her. All he kept thinking about was becoming a father, which was another reason why his date was so distracting.

With it being so early, luckily he was able to get on a 6:20 a.m. flight back to the Big Easy. What was even more exciting was Bryce finding a store in the terminal called Kids Works where he bought several baby gifts for Seven. He was particularly proud of a bib that read, *If You Think I'm Cute, Blame Daddy*, and couldn't wait to show it off.

"Sir, we're here," the taxi driver said breaking his thoughts.

"Damn, that was quick," Bryce said sitting up.

After paying the driver and giving him a decent tip Bryce walked up the steps to his apartment and slid his key into the knob. Once the dead bolt was unlocked, he gently pushed the door open before closing it behind him. Leaving his carry-on bag in the living room, he began walking down the hall with excitement about seeing his pregnant wife. But his excitement soon turned to curiosity when he heard Trey Songz singing, *Neighbors Know My Name* from inside the bathroom.

Damn, it's only 10:30. Seven doesn't normally get up until noon on Sundays, Bryce thought.

Figuring Seven wanted to start her day a little earlier, Bryce slowly opened the door thinking she would be inside singing along to the mini concert. However what he found almost took his breath away. Bryce's heartbeat instantly started racing when he saw Seven recording a naked man with a Flip Cam as he jerked off in the shower. His eyes increased three times their normal size when Bryce stepped further into the bathroom, and realized that the naked man was Stephon.

"What the fuck are you doing?" Bryce yelled.

When Seven looked back, it looked like she'd seen a ghost. "Oh my God. What are you doing here?"

"I live here. Why the fuck are you taping your brother

jerking off?" Bryce belted.

"Baby…please…just calm down," Seven said, placing the camera on top of the toilet seat. "I told Stephon about what we had going on and he wanted to be apart of…"

Bryce cut her off. "But he's your fucking brother."

"Man, chill the fuck out," Stephon said, stepping out the tub. He grabbed a towel and wrapped it around his waist.

"Stephon…please. Let me take care of this," Seven said standing between the two of them.

"What kind of sick shit are you into, Seven? You're his sister. I mean am I the only one who sees something wrong with this?" Bryce questioned.

"This shit ain't wrong because I'm not her real…"

"What are you doing home so soon?" Seven said, cutting Stephon off.

"You're not her real what?" Bryce said, ignoring Seven's question.

"I'm not her real brother." Stephon looked at Seven who looked like she was about to pass out. "Sorry, but I just can't hold this shit in anymore. She used to be my girl back in the day before she met your punk ass. But I guess from all the calls I get about money, she still needs big daddy."

Bryce didn't blink. He pushed Seven out the way and instantly started throwing punches. Stephon tried to block the blows as he fell back against the wall, but Bryce managed to over power him. Stephon was so busy trying to keep the towel in place, that his fighting skills seemed minimal. Seven screamed for Bryce to stop. She even tried to pull him away, but nothing worked. Enraged, Bryce continued to punch Stephon with his right hand that soon produced a bloody nose and mouth. The last punch Bryce threw sent Stephon straight to the floor.

"Get the fuck out!" Bryce roared before kicking Stephon in his rib cage.

Seven grabbed Bryce by both arms. "Bryce, please stop it. You're gonna hurt him."

"So fucking what? Are you taking up for this nigga?" Bryce snapped.

"No…not at all."

As they went back and forth, Stephon slowly stumbled to his feet, then took a fighting stance. "Let his punk ass go."

"Stephon, just get your stuff and leave!" Seven yelled. She quickly jumped between both men once again.

Blood dripped from Stephon's nose. "I'ma kill that muthafucka!"

"I'm right here!" Bryce barked.

"Stephon, don't make shit worse. Get your clothes. I'll call you later," Seven said.

Bryce looked at his wife sideways. "Oh really. You're gonna call him later."

Stephon stood there for a second. He realized that the battle was already lost, but the war had just begun. Grabbing his stuff off the bathroom floor, he quickly put his pants back on before heading to the door with his shirt and shoes in hand.

"This shit ain't over," Stephon warned just before opening the front door and slamming it shut.

"I can't believe this! How could you lie to me about him being your brother?" Bryce yelled.

"Well, he is like a brother to me now. We've known each other forever," Seven tried to explain.

"I don't care how long you've known him. People don't fuck their brother, Seven!"

"Baby, it's not what you think."

"How the fuck can you stand there and say some stupid shit like that? It's not what I think. I think you just fucked up because I saw Stephon jerking off in my shower with my wife taping him like some fake ass Tyler Perry!"

"Bryce, please just hear me out. While you were gone, I had this idea of doing a video promo ad to show clients what Black Tie Escorts has to offer, and I was planning on surprising you with the finished product when you got back."

Bryce paced back and forth opening and closing his fist.

"Black Tie Escorts, when the fuck did you name this shit? Besides, that nigga wasn't helping *me* out. He could've helped me out by not faking to be your brother for the past three years." Bryce felt so stupid for allowing them to play him like that.

"You're blowing this little thing way out of proportion. See, I knew you would act this way."

"If you knew I would act like this, why would you bring that motherfucka into our house and do that shit? If it was just a little thing then why didn't you tell me about your plans before I left? Why wait until I was out of town? Why keep this shit a secret just like your relationship with Stephon? I'll tell you why because you're a lying, money-hungry bitch."

Seven's face immediately turned to stone. She'd never heard Bryce call her out of her name, which quickly changed her demeanor. "No, I'm not a bitch. I'ma grown ass woman who doesn't need to ask anyone's permission to do what the fuck I want. Unlike you, I'm trying to create ways to keep us from being out on the street."

"Are you kidding me?" Bryce asked.

"Do you see me smiling? If the man I married had kept me in the lifestyle that I was used to, I wouldn't have to worry about anything but what time the mall opened."

"So, now all this shit is my fault."

"Well, it damn sure ain't my fault. I'm trying to change our situation around for the better. Everything I'm doing is for us," Seven replied.

"That reverse psychology shit won't work on me. You could've easily helped *us* out by getting a job that wouldn't disrespect our marriage. How could you do something like that? You're pregnant with my child!"

"I've already explained why I did it," Seven answered. "You weren't supposed to come back until later on this evening.

"Oh, so I ruined your plans, huh? If you weren't expecting me then what else were you planning on doing? I mean after Stephon jerked off, were y'all planning on fucking? Hell, did you fuck him last night?"

"I'm not going to dignify those accusations with a re-sponse," Seven replied.

"Yeah, I bet."

"So, where is the money from Chase?" Seven asked. "I see you came back early. Does that mean you fucked up another date?"

Bryce walked up on Seven with his hands clinched tight. "That's all you're ever concerned with. Forget the fact that I just caught you with a naked man. Seven is never wrong about any-thing, huh? You don't even have the decency to fucking apolo-gize."

"Look, you better calm down."

"You know what, I can't take anymore of this shit from you." Bryce walked past Seven and into the bedroom. Moments later, he started throwing clothes onto the bed mumbling one profanity after the next.

Seven stood at the bedroom door. "And where do you think you're going?"

"I can't stand to even look at you right now. I have to get out of here before some shit pops off that we'll both regret."

Seven ran up as Bryce walked to his closet and took out several shirts. "You're not going anywhere. We need to talk this shit out."

"It's nothing to talk about. I'm leaving and you're not going to stop me. You really fucked up this time."

Seven decided to call Bryce's bluff. "Well, you're not getting any of the money from the dates. If you're really leaving me then you're walking out that door with just the money in your pocket. How are you gonna get your raggedy-ass garage with that?"

Bryce didn't respond.

In the past three years, Bryce had never threatened to leave so Seven knew he must've been serious. "Baby please…okay you're right. Stephon should've never been here, and I'm sorry about that. I promise we didn't do anything. Please don't leave me. All this isn't good for the baby. What am

I suppose to do without you being here?"

Bryce stopped and glanced over at Seven. Even though her eyes were starting to fill up with tears, he continued to pull items from the closet. Once he was finished, he used the comforter to make a poor man's suitcase, tossed it over his shoulder and headed for the door.

"Oh my God! I feel a sharp pain in my stomach. Please don't go, I need you Bryce!" Seven yelled as she fell to her knees.

Bryce stopped. When he turned to see her crying on the floor, a part of him wanted to run back and comfort this wife, but the other part thought she was probably faking. "Save that bullshit. It won't work this time. Go ahead and finish doing your little video with that nigga. You know Angelique tried to warn me about your conniving ass!"

Chapter Nineteen

Bryce could hear Seven yelling as he stomped down the steps. However, before he could make it mid-way down the comforter got caught on the metal railing sending all his belonging onto the ground.

"Damn it!" Bryce yelled as he bent down to gather his stuff.

He thought the moment couldn't get any worse, but he was wrong. When he lifted his head, Bryce could see Ms. Medley walking over toward him.

"Y'all wake me up almost every damn morning. You know Bryce, you're way too sexy to go through this drama with that sorry ass excuse for a woman. You're the type of king who needs a woman who will cater to your every need. It hurts me to see you livin' on rock bottom when you have so much potential," Ms. Medley said bending down.

Bryce glanced up to see her swinging a pair of his boxer briefs on her finger. "I'm not in the mood for any of your shit right now." He snatched his underwear back.

"Does this bad attitude have anything to do with the half naked man I saw coming from your apartment a few minutes ago?"

"Look, you need to mind your business. What happens in my life is no concern of yours. You don't know me or my situation, you only think you do," Bryce said, picking up the rest of his clothes. He was surprised Seven hadn't come outside yet, and wanted to leave before she changed her mind.

"I know you still think about how I made you feel."

When Bryce glanced up at Ms. Medley, the flashback of their night together sent chills over his body.

"All I'm saying is that you shouldn't be wastin' your life with a woman who doesn't think of you the same way you think of her. I mean, I would never agree to you bein' with other women for money. I would work two, three jobs because sharin' you would be out of the question," Ms. Medley said helping him lift the bundle of clothes.

Deciding not to respond, Bryce walked over to the curb, and used his spare car key to pop the trunk to Seven's car.

"Get the fuck away from my car!" Seven belted from the living room window. She hadn't come outside, but she was obviously looking.

"I pay the car note anyway, so now it's my shit!" Bryce fired back. "Tell Stephon to buy you a new one."

After throwing the comforter inside, Bryce quickly hopped in the driver's seat and started the engine. By the time he pulled off, he could finally see Seven running outside and waving her arms. It looked like she was directing a plane to the runway.

"You can't take my car!" Seven yelled as he peeled down the street.

Bryce weaved his way through traffic at top speed. He broke several traffic laws as he made his way toward Mitch's house. Banging on the steering wheel, Bryce couldn't believe what had just happened. He needed to get to his boy's house quick before he killed someone. When Bryce pulled up to Mitch's spot twenty minutes later, he grabbed everything out of the trunk, then walked up and knocked on the door.

Mitch immediately broke out into laughter as soon as he saw Bryce standing in the doorway. "Let me guess, your woman threw your dumb ass out. What did Seven do, catch you with another broad?"

"Actually, I'm the one who left," Bryce said with a slight chuckle. Seconds later his chuckles turned into uncontrollable laughter.

"What's so funny?" Mitch asked. He moved to the side so Bryce could come in.

"It's just funny that your first thought would be that I was the one cheating and got caught. But in actuality, Seven was the one I caught with a dude this morning." Bryce walked into the living room and dropped the comforter on the floor.

Mitch closed the door. "You bullshitting. You caught her fucking another dude?"

"Not exactly like that, but I caught her filming Stephon while he was jerking off in my shower."

Mitch's mouth fell open. "Stephon…But I thought that nigga was her brother?"

"Me too. Turns out, he's not. That bitch has been lying the whole time."

"Oh shit. What did you do?"

Bryce sat down on the couch and began telling Mitch about the details of the fight.

"So, wait a minute. How did you catch the nigga trying to bust a nut in your shower? Where the fuck were you at?"

"It's a long story, but basically I was on my way back from New York. I was up there on a date that Seven set up for me." Bryce paused for a moment. "Seven goes out and finds women for me to sleep with."

Mitch started laughing again. "Bullshit, you expect me to believe that Seven goes out and finds other women for you to fuck. That's the dumbest thing I've ever heard. Don't take this the wrong way, but if that is the case, then you were living every man's fantasy. I know guys who would give their right nut to find a woman willing to do some shit like that. "

Bryce shook his head wondering if he should include the part about the money. "Nigga, didn't you just hear me tell you about Stephon? Why would I stay after seeing that shit? Besides, it's more complicated then that. Our arrangement wasn't as good as it sounds. You may think my life is a fantasy, but I'm living a fucking nightmare. She's only doing it because of the money anyway."

"What money?"

"Seven finds women who want to pay for an evening with me. If they want me to fuck them, she charges an additional fee," Bryce answered.

"Oh shit. So, basically you're a prostitute? How much do you make?" Mitch questioned with a huge grin.

"Not a prostitute…a male escort nigga," Bryce corrected. "Seven was charging $500.00 for sex and $300.00 if they just needed me to escort them to events and different functions."

"I don't recall the guidance counselor in high school ever telling us about those types of jobs being a possible career choice," Mitch giggled.

Bryce laughed as well. "If they did, the line would've been around the corner with dudes trying to sign up."

"So, were any of these broads old?" Mitch curiously asked. "I would love to make some extra money by fucking some lonely old ladies."

Mitch had gotten several laughs off of him already, so Bryce wasn't about to tell his boy about Ms. Medley. "Oh, these women aren't always old. They're a variety of ages, sizes, looks, and have different sexual appetites. I mean they're fine, sexy, classy and most of all…paid. Any man would jump through hoops to have them."

"What about any psycho bitches? You know…the kind that'll slice your tires, key your car or show up to your job announced," Mitch inquired.

"I haven't met any like that either. These women aren't looking for any emotional commitments. They just want to have fun and get their brains fucked senseless."

"Damn, I need to call Seven and see if she's hiring," Mitch joked.

"Nigga, you better be playing. I left her ass for a good

reason. I needed to get the fuck out of there before I did something real stupid."

Suddenly Mitch looked around the room. "That's a lot of clothes. How long are you planning on staying?"

"I just need to crash here for a little while until shit calms down. Is that okay? I know I didn't tell you that I was coming."

"Of course you can if it's just for a little while."

"What's that suppose to mean?" Bryce asked.

"You're my boy and I want us to stay that way. You can hang out here for a little bit, but if you're thinking of running away and moving up in here, then that shit ain't part of the solution. You're a good friend, but it would be hell to live with you," Mitch informed. "Besides, you wouldn't want to stay here. You'll never get any sleep with all the bitches I have running in and out of here."

"I'm not trying to run away from Seven. I just have to let both of us settle down. Right now all we're doing is yelling back and forth with neither one of us listening to the other. Besides, stop faking nigga. I know you don't have anybody coming through here except your mother."

"You got jokes, huh?"

Bryce took out several twenties from the money he made in New York and handed it to Mitch. "Man, you won't even know I'm here. I'll be at work most of the time anyway."

"I know you're here already," Mitch said taking the cash. "Look at my living room. Get your shit and take it upstairs."

Bryce laughed at his friend who'd always been a clean freak. After gathering his stuff and going into the guest room, he tossed his stuff in the corner and sat on the bed. Bryce pulled out his cell and realized he had several text messages from Seven. Turning off his phone, he fell back onto the bed, closed his eyes and wondered what his next move was going to be.

The other mechanics were surprised to see Bryce already at work and underneath a car when they arrived the next morning. It wasn't even his turn to open the garage. They made several jokes before going to work themselves. When Darrell walked into the garage a few minutes later to see if the Chevrolet Malibu was finished, he paused.

"Oh, look who's here. You're just the man I needed to see," Darrell said.

"Why? What's up?" Bryce asked.

"First things first, are you done with the Malibu? The owner will be here in twenty-five minutes to pick it up."

"Yeah, I saw the ticket on it. I put on the new starter and just finished rotating the tires," Bryce replied.

"Hey Jose, when the owner comes can you handle her? Bryce and I are going into my office to discuss some things. We're only to be disturbed for an emergency. Do you understand?" Darrell asked.

"Yeah, old man. I got you," Jose replied.

Bryce washed the dirt off of his hands, then followed Darrell in the back before sitting across from him.

"It's nice that you found your way back to work. You've been taking off quite a bit in the last few weeks. Plus when you do come, you're normally late. Is everything okay?" Darrell asked sitting behind his desk.

"I'm okay. My life is a little hectic right now, but I'm up for the challenge."

"That's nice to hear because I need your 'A' game. My wife had some complications and they admitted her into the hospital. They're gonna transport her to Baltimore tomorrow."

Bryce shook his head. "I have faith that everything will work out."

"Thank you. I called you back here because I need to know if you got the down payment for the garage," Darrell said. "Although I'm gonna be going back and forth to Baltimore for a minute, my plan is to leave New Orleans for good the second week in October."

Bryce looked at the calendar on the wall. "But that's two weeks."

"I know son, but I don't have any other choice."

"I don't have the money yet, but I'm working really hard."

"Well, Bryce I'm a little nervous about you getting it on time, so I'm gonna have to talk to a few other people. The owner from Precision Auto will probably be interested."

"I completely understand, but I'm still gonna try to get the money. You're just gonna have to be flexible with my schedule because I may need to work this other job in order to get the cash."

"Other job? I didn't know you were working somewhere else. Is that why you've been taking off so much? Why didn't you come and talk to me so we could work things out? What kind of work is it?" Darrell's questions wouldn't stop.

Bryce lowered his head. "Umm…it's a long story."

"Well, I can get the other guys to take care of the cars if you need some time off. I'm pulling for you. You go do what you have to so this place stays in the family," Darrell replied.

"Thank you. I won't let you down," Bryce said reaching over to shake Darrell's hand.

Darrel stood and walked around the desk with his arms open wide. "You're like a son. Give me a hug and not some business hand shake."

As the two men embraced, Bryce couldn't help but tear up as thoughts of how Darrell's constant support was parallel to his father's. It was a good feeling to know that somebody cared about him.

Bryce walked out of the office without a clue of how to get seventeen grand in fourteen days. The only thing that made that type of money was selling drugs or doing the escort thing, but there was no way he was going back to Seven with his tail tucked between his legs. He entertained the thought of doing it by himself.

When Bryce's cell phone rang, he thought it was a coincidence how Seven would be calling as soon as he thought about escorting on his own. She'd been calling, leaving messages and texting him repeatedly since he rolled out. Just to be safe, he'd parked her car a couple of blocks away in case she decided to show up at the garage. This time he decided to answer.

"Yeah."

"Hey Bryce, it's Angelique," her soft voice spoke.

He was surprised it wasn't Seven, but happy at the same time. "Hey Angelique, how have you been?"

"I'm fine and you?"

"I'm hanging in there. It seems like I'm down by one point with seconds left on the clock in a championship game."

"Wow…well if it's that bad why don't we meet for lunch at Meritage Restaurant inside the Boston Harbor Hotel? They have some excellent food and a good selection of wines."

"What time are you thinking?" Bryce asked.

"If you're up to it, I can go over to the restaurant and wait for you now."

"As much as I would love to, I can't leave work right now. I'm working on some cars and could really use the money."

"How much will you make if you stayed at work?"

The question caught Bryce off guard. "I guess I can make a few hundred, why?"

"How about you stop what you're doing and I'll pay you for your time. Actually, I'll pay double what you would make there. I really want to spend some more time with you. Plus, I signed a new client to the firm today and I don't have anyone to celebrate my good fortune with."

Angelique's offer blew Bryce away. "Are you sure?"

"One hundred percent."

"Let me think. A day with a beautiful, sexy woman or a day underneath broken cars covered in grease and dirt. Hmm…I think I'll take what's behind door number one," Bryce said with a loud laugh.

"So, is that a yes?"

"Yes, it is. Just give me about an hour though. I need to change before I get there."

"Then it's a date. I can't wait to see you again."

"I'm looking forward to seeing..."

Before Bryce could say another word suddenly a barrage of gunshots rang out inside the garage. He immediately dropped the phone and took cover like a trained solider. Bryce made sure his body was glued to the floor as several more shots rang out, causing all the windows to shatter. Seconds later, the rapid gun fire was replaced by the sound of tires peeling down the street. When he thought the coast was clear, Bryce hopped up and ran straight to Darrell's office to see if he was okay.

"D!" Bryce yelled when he saw his boss on the floor. He ran over and instantly checked for blood. "Are you okay?"

Darrell was obviously shaken up. "Yeah...yeah. I guess," he spoke in a soft tone. "What the hell happened?"

"Somebody shot into the garage. Let me go check on everyone else. I'll be right back!"

As Bryce ran toward the bay he wondered who could've been responsible for trying to take them out, but it didn't take long for one name to come to mind.

Chapter Twenty

By the time Bryce pulled onto Rue Toulouse Street and found a parking space in front of the hotel, it was eight o'clock. He'd spent the last six hours talking to police and the local news about the incident and trying to calm Darrell down. He was still disturbed about the episode himself. Despite the fact that he didn't have any proof, Bryce wanted to go track Stephon down to see if he was the trigger man. All witnesses could tell police was that they saw an old black Monte Carlo fleeing from the scene.

As the shooting continued to invade his thoughts, Bryce's cell phone began to ring. When he didn't answer, it continuously rang two more times back to back. Knowing it was Seven, he tried to ignore her constant harassment. But when he heard the chime indicting that he had a voicemail, Bryce finally decided to listen to what she had to say.

"Maybe she'll say something about Stephon," he said to himself. Bryce shook his head when the automated voice informed him there were twelve new messages.

"First message: *Oh my God. I saw the shooting on the news. Please call me back. I need to know that you're okay. I forgive you for leaving, now come home. All this isn't worth fighting about,*" Seven said.

Bryce quickly hit nine to delete the message. For some reason her sincerity sounded fake.

"Second message: *Bryce you're really starting to try my patience. It's bad enough that you left and aren't answering any of my calls, but look how you're treating me and the baby. What if something hap...*"

Bryce hit the nine again cutting the message short.

Knowing Seven was bound to say something that would mess up his mood, he decided not to listen anymore. Instead, he hopped out and made his way toward the hotel. He felt like a VIP when the older white doormen opened the door and greeted Bryce with a pleasant smile.

"Welcome to the Boston Harbor Hotel. Do you have any luggage, sir?"

"No, I'm just here to go to Meritage."

"Well, in that case, enjoy your meal, sir."

"Thank you," Bryce replied as he quickly walked into the foyer of the hotel.

When he made his way into the restaurant and up to the hostess, Bryce was already feeling anxious about seeing Angelique.

"Are you here to make a reservation for later this evening, sir?" the hostess asked.

"No, I'm actually meeting someone now," Bryce responded.

"May I have the name of your party?"

"Angelique Lyles," Bryce whispered like he was doing something illegal.

"Oh yes, she's right this way," the hostess said grabbing a menu.

Bryce looked around once they entered the dining area to find it completely empty with the exception of Angelique sitting at a rectangular table in the middle of the room. *Why the hell did the lady ask me what my parties name was if Angelique was the only person in here*, he wondered.

Angelique jumped up as soon as she saw him. "Oh my God, are you okay?" she asked giving him a huge hug. After finally getting in touch with Bryce when the call disconnected, she couldn't believe what happened.

"Yeah, I'm okay. It's been a crazy ass day." Hugging Angelique back, he pulled out his chair, then sat down.

"Yeah, I bet. So, do the police have any leads?"

"No, and I don't wanna talk about it. Let's just try to have a nice, early dinner now," Bryce responded. "I guess not too many people know about this place, huh?"

"Meritage is definitely open for dinner everyday, but because my firm is such a good customer, the owner had his chef close the place down just for this private date."

Bryce was beyond impressed. "Wow. I didn't know I was worth all the fuss."

"You're worth so much more so don't play yourself short," Angelique said with a wide smile.

"Have you decided on a selection, Ms. Lyles?" a waiter asked just before Bryce could respond.

"Well, how about we start with some fried scallops, and the crab salad. Then for my main course I'll have the maple smoked salmon," Angelique said.

The waiter looked at Bryce. "And for you, sir?"

"It all looks so good. I've never eaten here before. What would you recommend?" Bryce asked flipping through the menu.

"Everything is delicious, but I would recommend trying the braised short ribs with garlic potatoes or maybe the bacon seared pork tenderloin," the waiter replied.

"Okay, I'm sold. Let me try the short ribs and bring a bottle of Château Grand-Pontet for the table," Bryce responded.

"Excellent choice, sir," the waiter said picking up the menus.

"That's what I'm talking about. You handled that with so much class. Red wine goes perfect with beef. No circle is off limits to you," Angelique praised.

Over the next hour, Bryce felt so comfortable with Angelique as they ate and talked about everything from weather, to sports, and current events. However, their date was constantly interrupted by Bryce's phone.

"That's about the fifth time your phone has gone off without you answering it. Should I be worried about somebody looking for you?" Angelique asked in a jokingly manner.

Bryce pulled out his phone. It was Seven calling yet again. He pushed the ignore button and stuck the phone back into the holster on his waist. "It's nothing to worry about."

"Don't hold that stuff inside. It'll eat away at you until you lose it. It's always better to talk things out. Sometimes another person's perception can be helpful. I'm a very good listener."

"That was Seven."

"Oh. So, why aren't you answering? It's a bad idea to ignore your wife."

For some reason every time Bryce was around Angelique he felt extremely relaxed, like they'd known each other for years. He leaned forward, took her hand, then started telling Angelique everything that happened when he came home from New York. However, he left the part out about leaving Seven while she was pregnant. Deep down, he actually felt bad about that. When Bryce finished with the Seven drama, he moved on to the garage and his need for money in order to buy it.

"Hell if people are shooting the place up, maybe you should find another investment," Angelique said.

"I couldn't do that to my boss. He's been really trying to help me out."

"Well, I don't know what to say about your wife situation other than that's fucked up, but I can speak on the money part. What if I loan you the money? I could be like your silent partner," Angelique suggested.

"No, I need to do this for myself. You would own a portion of the business and that defeats the purpose."

"So, are you gonna go back to work for Seven? Is that how you're going to get the cash?"

Bryce quickly shook his head. "I seriously doubt it."

"Then work for me."

He stared at Angelique for a few seconds. "Work you for."

"Yeah. I could set you up with some of the women I've come across in my ventures. I know they would pay some major cash to be with you. That is, if you wouldn't mind me helping out a friend."

"I don't know about that," Bryce responded with an uneasy expression.

"Look, I'm not trying to take Seven's place, but I can help you make some money. Your wife meant well, but she only knew certain types of blue collar, working class women. I know women who'll pay what she's asking for on shoes and belts."

Bryce continued to shake his head. "I still don't know. I honestly don't wanna go back to doing that shit."

"Anything for dessert?" the waiter asked.

"What I plan to have for desert isn't on your menu. Just put everything along with a twenty-five percent tip on my corporate card and send some champagne up to the Presidential Suite."

The waiter blushed. "Certainly madam, and thank you for the gracious tip."

Bryce got up and pulled Angelique's chair back, then helped her to her feet. She locked her arm around his waist and headed for the front desk. Angelique didn't even have to say anything as the Spanish looking gentleman handed her a room key.

"Damn, I need to be rolling like you one day," Bryce said as they pushed the button on the elevator.

"Well, if things go according to plan maybe you will."

When they finally made it to the Presidential Suite, Bryce held up Angelique's hand and kissed it. "I guess I'll say good-bye now."

"Where are you going? I got this room for us. I was hoping to be your first client since you're on your own now. Besides, now you won't have to split the money with Seven," Angelique said, pulling Bryce into the room.

"Was this your plan all along? Did you ask me to come here so you could get me in the sack? I feel dirty yet honored," Bryce joked.

"Yes, and obviously my plan worked because you're here," Angelique replied. "I'm going to the bathroom to remove my clothes, and freshen up. When I get out I pray to find you naked with your dick hard as a fucking missile."

Bryce was getting ready to speak, but Angelique placed her finger over his lips. She then switched her thick juicy ass into the bathroom and shut the door. Bryce stood frozen.

How do I get myself in situations like this, he wondered.

Angelique emerged from the bathroom a few minutes later to find the curtains drawn, and the sultry sounds of *If Only For One Night* by Luther Vandross playing on the hotel radio. Angelique walked over to the bed wrapped in a white towel and smiled as Bryce's eyes made contact with hers. She then unfastened the hair clip holding her long weave, placed it on the night stand then allowed the long locks to fall across her back and shoulders. The sheets gave Bryce's naked body chills as he scooted over and took position in front of Angelique. After reaching his hand up to pull off the towel, Bryce paused to admire just how beautiful she was.

At that moment something seemed really different about her. As Angelique got closer, his heart rate began to increase and goose bumps formed on his arms. Bryce couldn't explain it. All he knew is that he wanted Angelique bad.

She leaned down to allow her lips to be close enough for him to taste. The first kiss was quick and just a tease as Angelique pulled her head back. Moments later, Bryce grabbed Angelique and pulled her onto the bed to ensure she wouldn't do that again on their next embrace. He pressed his lips against hers while holding her head with one hand and rubbing her back with the other. Soon, her soft pants turned to sweet moans. She loved the way his tongue explored her mouth.

Angelique pushed him off to catch her breath. "How long do I get to have you?"

"Depends on just how much money you're planning on spending," Bryce answered with a quick laugh.

"Oh, it's like that. Well, in that case I better get my money's worth."

"I come with a money back guarantee if I don't exceed your every expectation."

All of a sudden, Angelique pushed Bryce's head in the direction of her wanting pussy. "If this is on my dime, then I need you to start with eating me like it's your last meal."

Bryce didn't hesitate. He locked his hands around Angelique's waist, used his shoulders to open her thighs and dove his face into her sweet canel. Bryce pulled her hanging lips into his mouth sucking faster until he felt her back rising. He then used his fingers to massage her thighs as his tongue splashed inside her overflowing vagina.

Bryce continued this for several minutes until Angelique's sensations became too much for her to bear. She tried to move her body around the bed to unlock his flicking tongue, but Bryce remained locked on her pussy with the strength of a full grown pit-bull. Seconds later, Angelique filled Bryce's mouth with an explosion of warm, thick cum.

"I've had enough. I can't take anymore," Angelique said, still trying to detach his lips.

However, Bryce refused to stop. He continued to twirl his tongue deeper inside her overflowing pussy until his goatee and chin dripped with juices. Bryce looked as if he'd been hit in the face with a custard pie when he finally released her lower back and came up for air.

"Is this what you wanted?" he asked crawling up Angelique's shaking body.

"Don't touch me. Oh my God, I've never had my pussy eaten like that before."

Not following directions, Bryce slid his hand down and began massaging her clit in a circular motion. He felt her body trembling as his fingers slid back and forth. Angelique pretended she needed him to stop, but really didn't put up much of a fight. Bryce slowly slid finger after finger inside her walls until he had four of them moving in and out as his thumb clapped the tip of her vagina. Just then, Angelique shook her head frantically and shot out another gusher of her womanly juices.

Moments later, she tried desperately to catch her breath. "I'm at a lost for words right now."

"So, did you get your money's worth?" Bryce asked.

Angelique shook her head. "Absolutely."

They both sat in silence for a few more minutes until Bryce suddenly gave her a serious look. "I really need to make some money, so I'm gonna allow you to set me up on a few escorts with some of your friends," he uttered. "But it's just until I get enough money to give my boss for the garage."

Angelique smiled. "I'm so glad you decided to let me help you. I want to be that woman who you can count on. I'll tell you what, I won't even take any of the money you make."

"No, I couldn't do that."

"I insist. It'll give you a chance to really save."

"Well, how about this...let me go on a few dates, then give my boss some cash to try and hold him off. From there I'll start giving you a portion."

"I guess that's fair. I'll make some calls tonight. I have the perfect woman in mind. She's loaded and always looking for a good time. How's tomorrow?" Angelique questioned.

"Tomorrow."

"Is that too soon? I thought you needed to make the money fast. Hell, I thought about starting tonight, but figured that would be too much."

"No, you're right. I'm short for time. I need to get this money train moving at top speed, so tomorrow is cool," Bryce answered.

"Where are you staying?"

"I'm staying with my man Mitch."

"No, that won't do. The fact that you're someone's roommate right now seems juvenile. Not to mention, some of my friends are really known women, so hotels will be out, too. It won't play out right if you take them back to some dirty house."

"Mitch has a nice place. It's not a mansion, but the bed is big enough to do the job," Bryce replied.

"The apartment my firm put me in when I first moved here is still paid for through the end of next month. Why don't you stay there and use it for your clients?" Angelique suggested.

"Are you sure?"

"Yes. It's not a big deal."

"Damn, I can't believe you're willing to do all of this for me when we basically just met."

"Hey, unlike your wife, I'm really trying to help you out." Bryce got quiet for a minute, and didn't respond. "So, let me ask you something. How did you get past your wife's previous job as an escort when you married her? Most men would've been a little turned off by that."

Bryce laughed. "Who told you that? Seven was a stripper, not an escort."

Angelique displayed a slight grin when she realized the information was new to him. "Are you sure? My cousin Hypnotic told me that she knew Seven from the escort service they both worked at."

Bryce's eyebrows crinkled. "Hypnotic. You mean the girl from Temptations? Yeah, see you must have it wrong. They were both strippers at the same time, but not escorts. Naw, I would've never married a damn prostitute."

"Yeah, you're right. Maybe I just misunderstood. You know your wife better than me," Angelique replied.

It looked like Bryce was in deep thought. "I want, no I need for you to call your cousin right now," he finally said.

"No, Bryce just forget I ever said anything. I'm sure I have it wrong."

"Call her," he demanded.

Quickly grabbing her phone, Angelique called Hypnotic who confirmed Seven's undisclosed occupation. Bryce had finally reached his 'last straw', and couldn't wait to end things with Seven indefinitely. Finding out about his wife's secrets made his moment with Angelique even better.

Chapter **Twenty-One**

While Bryce and Angelique enjoyed each other's company, Seven was furious that she had to catch a cab down to the strip club. With Bryce refusing to call her back, she was in a terrible mood. Even Stephon was MIA. After throwing her money toward the driver, she jumped out and slammed the door. As Seven power walked to the front door, she mumbled all sorts of profanities which were geared toward her husband.

"I'll show his bitch ass," she said.

"What's going on, Seven?" the bouncer asked.

"Get the hell out my way, Niko," Seven shot back as she stormed past him and held up her right hand.

"Damn, I was just speaking," Niko said as he watched Seven shake her voluptuous ass into the club.

When she walked through the huge black curtains, Seven stood there looking around the club until she noticed him over in the V.I.P. lounge. She marched over, ignoring the men reaching out their hands and asking for a lap dance.

"Where the fuck is he?" Seven shouted when she got to the bar.

Mitch looked up to see Seven standing with her hands on her hips. "What are you talking about? Who is *he*? Speedy?"

"Don't play fucking games with me. You know who I'm talking about. Where's Bryce?"

"I don't know. Maybe I should be asking your cheating

ass. Thank God nobody got hurt in that garage today. You probably got that nigga Stephon to do it."

"I didn't get Stephon to do shit. I'm just as surprised to hear about it as you are," Seven responded. "So, where is he?"

"As you can see we're not connected at the hip, so I don't know."

"Does it look like I'm in the mood to play games? You better tell me where Bryce is or I swear to God, I'll fuck your whole world up!" Seven shouted over the loud music.

The guys at the bar focused on the two of them go at it.

"Look, I'm working. Besides, you know I wouldn't tell you where Bryce was even if I did know," Mitch responded. "I heard about the little business y'all got going on. Why don't you go back to that part of your life if you need money? I'm sure they have room for you tonight." Mitch pointed to the stage.

"Why use my fucking body when he can use his? Besides, it's not about me going back to strip anymore. It's about him taking care of me."

Mitch gave her a disgusted expression.

"What the fuck are y'all looking at? All the pussy is that way!" Seven shouted at the men looking in her direction. When they finally turned around, she directed her anger back toward Mitch. "Now, I'm gonna ask your ass one more time to tell me where he is or else."

Mitch laughed. "Or else what?"

"So you really wanna be cocky right now and play dumb, huh? You must really think I'm joking," Seven fired back. "You know I think a lot of niggas in here would love to find out what type of guy you really are," she said leaning closer to the bar.

Suddenly Mitch's smile faded.

"Oh, I see I finally got your attention, huh?" This time Seven laughed. "Why didn't I get my payment from you the other day? You didn't even answer the phone when I tried to remind you about the shit."

Mitch looked around the club. "Because Seven, I'm tired of paying you. You're one of the reasons why I work so hard in the first place. It's not right what you're doing."

"No, what's not right is the fact that you like licking balls instead of licking pussy."

One of the guys sitting at the bar glanced over at Mitch. Completely enraged, Mitch started shaking his head then grabbed Seven by the arm. He quickly pulled her down to the other end of the bar where no one was sitting.

"Have you lost your fucking mind?" he asked.

Seven snatched her arm away. "Don't get mad at me because you're gay. Maybe you should've thought about that before I caught your ass sucking some dude's dick in the back of the club that night." She smiled again. "How do you think the guys at the construction site would feel if they knew you were a faggot? How do you think Bryce would feel?"

Mitch looked around again. "You need to shut the fuck up."

"No. Did you think I was gonna let you get away with not paying me? Every week…that's our arrangement. Secrets cost money, muthafucka."

"So, you decided to come to my job and shake me down?"

"No, actually I came so you could tell me where my fucking husband is. If you don't tell me then I'm gonna make sure all these people up in here know that you like being fucked up the ass like a little bitch. Your secret will no longer be safe until you give me what I want."

Mitch let out a long sigh. "Bryce came over to my house. He's crashing in my guest room, but I can't tell you where he is right now. I haven't talked to him since the garage incident."

"Is he fucking somebody else? I mean seriously. Not the date shit."

"I don't know that either."

"Well, when you see my husband, you better get in his ear and convince him to bring his black ass home. Me and the baby need him." She rubbed her stomach as Mitch looked on.

"I would really hate to find out that you're poisoning him with some bad shit about me fruit cake." When Seven turned to leave, she stopped and turned back around. "Oh, and get your money together because I'll need a payment soon."

Seven didn't sleep at all. After calling Bryce's cell phone all night until he finally turned it off, she barely got any rest while wondering where he could be. Or worse, who he was with. She even convinced one of the girls at the strip club to give her a ride over to Mitch's house so she could hopefully catch Bryce walking in or out, but he never did.

When Seven walked into the salon, she was surprised to see every chair in the waiting area completely full. Camille gave her a sharp stare as she walked over to get her black smock from the rack.

"Oh, so you finally decided to show up to work today. Ce-Ce is pregnant and she comes more than you do. You better be glad I need your ass, or you could walk right back out the door," Camille started to vent.

"Yeah girl, where you been?" Ce-Ce cosigned from the other side of the room.

Little did Camille know the only reason why Seven was there to begin with was to try and get her mind off of Bryce. She was so busy worrying about him that she hadn't put any effort into the escorting business or her personal appearance. As Seven put on her smock, she could see everyone staring at her dusty Crocs and dingy grey sweat pants.

"Who's next?" she asked ignoring all the looks.

When a large woman stood up, Seven directed her over to the shampoo bowl. However, before she could even turn the water on, Seven's cell phone started ringing. Her eyes lit up like Christmas lights when she pulled it out. It was Bryce.

"It took you long enough to call me back. Where are you?" Seven asked trying to hold back her excitement.

"Don't worry about where I am. I just called to tell you to lose my fucking number."

"Bryce look…"

He instantly cut her off. "Shut the fuck up. All you do is lie, so I'm sick of hearing your mouth. I can't believe you never told me that you used to be an escort. Don't you think I had a right to know that shit?" Bryce roared.

Seven's eyes widened, but she had to keep her cool. "What are you talking about? Why don't you tell me where you are so we can meet and talk this out?"

"I'm not meeting you anywhere, liar. Now that I think about it, I don't think you've ever told me the truth about anything. I bet you're lying about being pregnant, too."

"How could you say something like that? I love you, Bryce," Seven replied.

"I don't think you even know what that word means."

"Please meet me at home so we can work this out. I don't know who or what has polluted your mind with such negative thoughts about me, but we need to talk about it," Seven pleaded. She could care less about who heard her conversation.

"I don't know if I'm ever coming home. When I think of you, only thoughts of how many lies you've probably told me pops up. I can't trust anything you say," he said before hanging up.

Seven quickly dialed Bryce's number back, but it went straight to voicemail. She tried several more times, but again the same thing happened. As Seven began to pace the floor, she walked past the front window when suddenly a car caught her eye. She instantly froze as the vehicle parked across the street from the shop.

Hold up…that looks exactly like the car that picked Bryce up outside the swinger's party, Seven thought staring even harder.

Seven was so busy waiting to see who emerged from the driver's side that she didn't hear Camille calling her name

"Seven, go wash the client's hair. She's waiting,"

Camille said.

Seven turned in Camille's direction and held up her index finger. "Just give me five minutes."

"No, do it now!" Camille fired back. "She's waited long enough."

Suddenly the chimes on the front door sounded as Angelique stepped inside the salon. As always she was dressed from head to toe. "Hello everyone," she greeted.

Everyone in the salon turned around, including Seven who became enraged. She instantly remembered Bryce saying something about listening to Angelique when he stomped out the door.

"Where the fuck is my husband?" Seven shouted.

A surprised look came over Angelique's face. "Excuse me."

"Don't play that shit with me. I saw you outside the swinger's party that night. I know Bryce got into your car. Where did you take him?"

Every eye in the salon was pointed in their direction.

"I'm not sure what you're talking about. I really think you have me confused with someone else. I don't know where your husband is. I used him for our prearranged event that time, but nothing else. If you've lost your husband then maybe you should call the police and place a missing persons report," Angelique said.

"Bitch, who do you think you're talking to? I'm not going to ask you again. You better tell me where Bryce is or I'm gonna whip your ass!" Seven shouted.

All the customers in the salon sat on the edge of their seats. They felt like they were watching a real life taping of *Basketball Wives*. Camille realized that she needed to do something before the two of them moved from verbal threats to full contact.

"I need both of you to calm down. This is not the time or place to have this discussion. I'm running a place of business," Camille said stepping between the two staring women.

Angelique turned to Camille. "I know, that's why I'm here. Is it too late to get my hair done?"

Seven quickly moved her head back and forth. "Oh hell no. You're not getting your hair done here." She looked at Camille. "I'm not washing her fucking hair."

"I hope all your employees don't act like this," Angelique said.

When Seven started walking toward Angelique, Camille quickly grabbed her arm, then pushed her toward the back of the salon. The customers were mumbling for Camille to let Seven go.

"She knows where her husband is. Let Seven go so she can beat it out of her!" one customer shouted.

"Everyone, just sit back. I apologize for this little episode," Camille stated.

As Angelique stood there watching Camille and Seven, her cell phone started ringing. When she looked at the number, a huge smile crept over her face. Angelique quickly placed the phone to her ear. "Girl, I've been calling you all morning."

"I saw your number on my phone, but I've been at Saks forever. You know I don't like to be disturbed when I shop. What's going on?" the woman asked.

"What's on your agenda for tonight, Jayda? I think I might have something that you'll be interested in," Angelique responded.

"Nothing major. Thank God my boring ass husband has to fly to California for an urgent meeting, so I'll be home all by myself."

Angelique smiled. "Well, this is fate then because I've got a number for an amazing male escort who can come by and keep you company. Trust me, I've used him before and he's well worth it," Angelique added.

Seven couldn't believe her ears. *I know that bitch ain't got the audacity to set up a date with my husband right in front of my face.*

Angelique nodded her head a few times as she listened

to Jayda's response. "Okay, I'll call you back with the details once I finish with my hair appointment. You need to make arrangements because his services aren't cheap and he doesn't accept credit cards," she said with a laugh, then hung up.

"Oh, hell no. Camille, please move," Seven said as Angelique walked over to the waiting area and sat down.

"Umm…Miss. Camille never said if she could take you," Cee Cee chimed in.

"Were you setting up a date for Bryce?" Seven questioned.

Ignoring everyone, Angelique picked up a magazine and leaned back.

"Bitch, I know you heard me talking to you. I asked if you were setting up a date for Bryce," Seven repeated.

Angelique finally looked up. "Maybe…maybe not."

Suddenly, Seven rushed over to Angelique and smacked the magazine out of her hand. In return, Angelique jumped up and pushed Seven away.

"Have you lost your mind? Don't put your hands on me!" Angelique yelled.

"I'm looking for Bryce and you seem to be the only one that knows where the hell he is. I'll do more than just put my hands on you if you don't tell me where he is," Seven fired back.

"I'm not your husband's keeper. If you can't keep up with your man, maybe he was never yours in the first place," Angelique responded. "Sounds like to me you're just mad because your free ride is over."

Before anyone knew it, Seven leapt forward and punched Angelique directly in her face. The entire salon gasped for air as Camille let out a loud shriek.

"Where the fuck is Bryce?" Seven yelled.

Angelique placed her hand on her cheek. She was stunned.

However, before Angelique could retaliate, both Camille and Cee Cee ran over and grabbed the women. Camille grabbed

Angelique by her shoulders while Cee Cee pulled Seven by her arm. Seven kept trying to kick Angelique as Cee Cee dragged her across the salon.

"I'll kill you!" Seven belted as she tried to break free from Cee Cee's grip.

"Seven, I need you to calm down. I'm pregnant. You are going to hurt me, you and my baby if you keep this up," Cee Cee said.

"Cee Cee, let me go, so I can kill that bitch!" Seven screamed.

"Do you think this is going to bring your husband back? You're just a female pimp who's mad because her money maker finally grew a brain and realized that you don't care about him and never did," Angelique spoke.

"You're talking like you know me. Bitch, you just moved here. You don't know anything about me or my relationship with my husband. I love my husband and he loves me," Seven said snatching away from Cee Cee.

"Bryce doesn't want to see you. He's mad and that was made very clear to me all night long," Angelique quickly shot back.

"Oh, hell no. That bitch went too far with that. You need to handle that shit and fuck her up!" a customer yelled out.

"I'm not going to stay here and get into a street fight with a woman that's nowhere near my level. I'll just take comfort in lying in your man's arm tonight," Angelique said before walking toward the front door.

"Don't let that bitch out. I'm going to fuck you up," Seven said, trying to get over to Angelique as Camille blocked her. "This ain't over! I'll be seeing you real soon."

"I'm looking forward to it," Angelique replied. "Oh, one last thing…is there any position you want me to fuck Bryce in tonight," Angelique said just before walking out.

That bitch picked the wrong woman to fuck with. I'll make her regret the day she ever came to New Orleans, Seven thought as everyone in the salon started mumbling.

BEDROOM GANGSTA

Chapter Twenty-Two

Angelique drove straight over to the apartment where Bryce was staying. As soon as she walked into the bedroom and realized he was asleep, she tip-toed over to the edge of the bed and sat down. Bryce rolled over a few seconds later and instantly became concerned after noticing the mark on her face. He quickly sat up.

"Oh shit, what happened to you? I thought you were getting your hair done today?"

Angelique shook her head. She thought about telling him about her altercation with Seven, but decided it served no purpose at that moment. "I didn't see a customer coming into the salon when I was trying to leave, so the door smacked me in the face."

"Baby, you need to be more careful," Bryce said rubbing her cheek. "Does it hurt?"

Before Angelique could respond, Bryce's cell phone started ringing. He reached over and retrieved it from the night stand. Bryce was expecting it to be yet another call from Seven, but to his surprise it was Mitch. "What up, nigga?"

"Hey man, I need to holla at you. Are you busy?" Mitch said.

"Kind of."

"Well, this is important. All I need is five minutes,"

Mitch informed.

"Hey, Mitch needs to talk to me. Can we finish our conversation in a few minutes?" Bryce asked Angelique.

Angelique kissed his forehead. "Sure, I need to use the bathroom anyway. Take your time."

Bryce watched as she got up from the bed and switched toward the bathroom. When Angelique looked back, the grin on Bryce's face told the whole story. He was definitely falling for her.

"Bryce, you there? Bryce," Mitch spoke into the phone.

Mitch's voice broke Angelique's and Bryce's stare. "My bad, I'm still here. What's going on?"

"Was that Seven you were just talking to?"

"Hell no. I'm not dealing with that lying bitch anymore."

"Oh, so who was that?"

"It's nobody you know," Bryce informed.

"So, where are you?"

"At a friend's. Can you tell me what's up?" Bryce spoke with a rushed tone.

"Well, I called to tell you that Seven came down to the club last night."

"Oh really. What, she decided to go back to work? Typical."

"Bryce, I need you to listen to me. I've known you all your life. We've been through so much and I've never steered you wrong. I really think you should go back home. Seven was really expressing her love for you this time. She was actually sincere with tears and everything."

Bryce looked at the phone before placing it back to his ear. "Who the hell is this? This can't be Mitch. You've never liked Seven and you hated the fact that I married her. Now just because she showed up crying, that changed your entire take on her."

"It was one of those moments that you had to be there to really understand. Seven is hurting and it's because she really loves you. I thought maybe all she cared about is money, but last night I saw a different side," Mitch declared.

"I don't care how upset Seven seemed. I'm not going back home. Do you know I found out that she used to be an escort?" Bryce laughed. "I mean, don't you think her being a stripper was bad enough. Come on man…that's basically a prostitute."

"Well, you're one now, so how can you judge her," Mitch responded.

"I can't believe you're taking up for her. You should be on my side."

Angelique stood in the bathroom listening to Bryce's every word. Even though it was clear that Bryce had left Seven on his own. She was going to make sure that he never went back.

"Look, you really need to take your ass home. She's pregnant. Don't run out on her now," Mitch responded.

"I love you like a brother, but you need to stay out of this one. I'll be okay."

"Well, if that's the case, then I'm not going to be your crutch. You can't stay at my house when I know you need to be at home with a woman who loves you."

Bryce pulled down the phone from his ear and stared at it as if he could see Mitch. "If that's how you feel, then I'll come by to get my shit asap," he said hanging up.

As soon as Bryce fell back onto the bed, the bathroom door slowly opened. When Angelique appeared, her eyes were red, puffy and had tears streaming down both cheeks. Bryce quickly sat back up.

"What's wrong?"

"I wasn't going to tell you this, but today at the salon." Angelique started crying even harder.

"What happened at the salon?" Mitch asked.

"When I went to get my hair done in Camille's salon, Seven started asking me all these questions about you. When I didn't give her the answers that she wanted to hear, she attacked me. I tried to defend myself, but the other women in the shop joined in and jumped me," Angelique said covering her face with her hands. As a lawyer, lying was her specialty.

Bryce got up and walked over toward her. "Baby, I'm so sorry that I got you mixed up in all of this."

"It's not your fault. I'm just upset at how my face looks," Angelique said peeking through her fingers to see his response.

"I still think you're the prettiest woman I've ever seen," Bryce replied. "Now, let's change the topic. We shouldn't give Seven any more power by talking about her. So, what's up with the escort for tonight?" he asked wiping her crocodile tears.

"Yes, you'll be escorting my friend Jayda. She's a beautiful pediatrician who's looking for a good time and open for anything. She's also married to a rich real estate developer, but don't worry, her husband is out of town.

"Wait…wait. She's married. The last time Seven set me up on a date with a married chick, he came home and almost caught me."

Angelique gave him a seductive look. "Well, I'm not Seven. She's not even in my league so don't worry about that. If your date goes well like I know it will, by this time tomorrow, there will be forty to fifty messages on my phone."

Bryce decided to go with his new tan slacks that he'd ran out and bought along with a powder blue shirt for the date. After putting on the shoes, he splashed a little cologne on his neck and headed out the door. As one of the street lights in front of the building flickered, Bryce clicked the button on Seven's car alarm, slid behind the wheel, then drove off down the street.

He rode in silence until he got to a stop light, and his phone rang. Looking down at the number, he started not to answer. But a part of him wanted to know what he had to say.

"What's up?"

"Slim, I was out of line. How about we meet up at the club and I'll make us a couple of shots to clear the bad blood from our conversation earlier," Mitch replied.

"Man, it's cool, but you sounded real gay."

Mitch became silent. He began to worry if Bryce had already talked to Seven and she told him about his little secret. "What are you talking about? Who you calling gay?"

"That's what I'm talking about. You seem real sensitive with everything. First, you hate Seven then you become her advocate. Second, you call me to tell me to go home, then get freaked out when I tell you that I'm good. Damn, calm down. Are you on your fucking period?" Bryce asked with a huge laugh.

"Fuck you, nigga!"

Bryce laughed. "Awe, did I hurt your feelings?"

"Let's change the subject before I have to whip your ass when I see you. You coming down to the club to get that drink," Mitch asked.

"No, tonight is not a good time. I got a job to do."

Mitch was about to ask Bryce about the job when Bryce's cell phone beeped. Bryce put Mitch on hold. "Hey you," he answered.

"Hey, I forgot to tell you where you'll be meeting Jayda," Angelique replied. "She wants to meet you at a hotel in Metairie."

"Oh yeah, that's right. I'm so dumb that I got in the car not realizing I didn't have a destination. Hold up, let me write the address down just in case I'm not familiar with the area." Bryce pulled over and took a napkin out of Seven's glove compartment, then grabbed a pen off the floor. "I'm ready."

As Bryce wrote everything down, he was so concerned with getting the address right that he never noticed a police car pulling up behind him. Moments later, the officer tapped on his window, which caught Bryce by surprise.

"Is there a problem officer?" Bryce said rolling down the window.

"I need your driver's license and registration," the police officer responded.

"Did I pull over in a bad spot? I was just writing something down. I'll move right now."

"License and registration, sir," the police office said again.

Bryce reached back into the glove compartment and retrieved the registration. He then opened his wallet and got his driver's license. When Bryce handed it out of the window, the officer grabbed both items and walked back to his squad car.

"You won't believe what's happening to me right now," Bryce said into the phone.

"I heard. Are you parked illegally or something?" Angelique inquired.

"I have no idea, but let me call you right back." After hanging up, Bryce watched the officer in his rearview. It felt like he'd been waiting forever when the officer finally returned to his window. "So, how much is my bill," Bryce said trying to be funny.

"I need you to step out the car, sir."

Bryce quickly changed his tone. "Okay, what's going on?"

"I said, get out the car now!" the officer said in a more commanding voice.

Bryce quickly opened the door and got out. "What did I do?"

"Turn around and put your hands on the hood. This car was reported stolen."

"What? No…wait. There must be some kind of mistake. This is my wife's car. I didn't steal it!" Bryce began shouting.

"You have the right to remain silent, and I suggest you exercise that right," the police officer said as he continued to read Bryce his rights."

Moments later, the officer walked Bryce to his squad car, opened the door, then pushed him into the back seat. "This is some bullshit," Bryce said right as they pulled off.

Chapter Twenty-Three

Bryce paced the dirty floor of the holding cell wondering when Angelique was going to come get him. It seemed like he'd been there for days when only three hours had passed. When the iron bars finally slid open, everybody in the cell with Bryce looked up.

"Deans…you're outta here," the officer on duty said.

"Thank God," Bryce said under his breath as he walked out of the cell.

He followed the officer up the stairs and out to the precinct's processing area before a huge smile shot across his face. He was so happy to see Angelique standing next to a well-dressed man holding a black leather briefcase. The officer walked Bryce over to the desk so he could retrieve his belongings.

"I'm so glad you didn't leave me in here. Thank you," Bryce said, giving Angelique a massive hug.

"Are you kidding? I would've never left you in this place." She turned to the other guy. "Bryce, this is Adrian Wilson. He's a top criminal defense attorney in New Orleans. He pulled a few strings to get you out of here without any charges filed."

Bryce shook Adrian's hand. "Thanks, Mr. Wilson. I thought I was gonna have to spend a few nights in here until they cleared up this misunderstanding."

"No problem, Bryce. Apparently, your wife really needed her car. She rushed down and picked it up right before the impound lot closed."

Yeah that sounds like her, Bryce thought.

"We'll talk about this some other time. Right now we've gotta go," Angelique butted in. "Adrian thanks again. I owe you one now." As Angelique and Bryce hurried out of the station, she filled him in on the details. "We have to hurry. Even though you're super late, Jayda is still willing to see you."

At that moment, Angelique's behavior reminded Bryce of Seven, but he decided to disregard it. Besides, he wasn't going to make any money if Jayda didn't pass the word, so Bryce had to make sure he showed up. After jumping in the car, Angelique drove straight to the hotel where Jayda was waiting.

"I can't believe Seven called her car in stolen."

"Why not? Can't you see she's a bitch who's just trying to get back at you?" Angelique said in a stern voice. "I just don't want you to let this foolishness get in the way of this date. Luckily Adrian got you off, so let's move on."

"I think after this date I better give my boss some money so he'll know I'm working on it."

"That's not a bad idea," she agreed.

Fifteen minutes later, Angelique pulled over and double parked in front of the Sheraton on Galleria Blvd. "You owe me big time," she said leaning over to kiss Bryce.

"Don't worry, I'll save some energy and work off part of my debt when I'm done with this date," Bryce replied just before kissing her back.

"Jayda is gonna drop you off at the apartment when you all are done. I have a big meeting at the firm tomorrow morning, so I'm gonna go home and get some rest. You can make it up to me later."

"No problem. Thanks again," Bryce said before getting out the car.

As he walked inside and Angelique pulled off, neither

one of them knew that Seven was secretly parked across the street. She'd been out there since leaving the impound lot and finding the napkin Bryce wrote on.

"I knew that bitch was setting him up on a date earlier," she said.

Trying to catch Bryce before he got too far, Seven quickly jumped out of the car and ran inside. But by the time she made it to the lobby, Bryce was nowhere to be found. Seven walked over to the desk.

"Good evening Miss, may I help you?" the guy behind the desk asked.

"Can you tell me what room Bryce Deans is in, please?" Seven responded.

"I'm sorry Ma'am, but we're not allowed to give out room information."

"Well, can you at least call up to the room for me? I really need to talk to him."

The clerk looked on his computer. "I'm sorry but we don't have a Bryce Deans registered. Is there anything else I can help you with?"

"Did you see the man with the bald head and goatee who just walked in about five or ten minutes ago? I need to know what room he's in. I'm supposed to be the third part of a very kinky sex triangle."

The clerk gave Seven a crazy look. "Well, if that's the case then you should know how to find the room number without me giving it to you. Now, do you need anything else?"

"No, I don't," she said walking off.

Seven didn't know what to do other than going from floor to floor until she found her husband. After getting on the elevator, she started on the second then slowly worked her way up. Seven walked down each corridor dialing Bryce's cell hoping to hear his Jay-Z ring tone. She also hoped that he didn't have his phone on vibrate or turned it off before she found him. While walking on the eighth floor, Seven suddenly stopped in front of room 824 when she heard the famous rapper's lyrics.

She quickly hung up, then called the phone again just to make sure she had the right room.

Presidents to represent me.

I'm out for Presidents to represent me.

I'm out for Dead Presidents to represent me.

Seven started banging on the door and screaming to the top of her lungs "Bryce, open this damn door. I know you're in there!"

"What the fuck?" Bryce said as he walked over to the door. *How the fuck did she find me,* he wondered while looking through the peep hole.

"Who is that?" Jayda asked walking up behind him.

Bryce put his finger against her lips to keep her quiet. "It's my wife," he whispered.

"Get rid of her now. I can't be involved in any drama," Jayda said.

"I hear you talking, Bryce. Open this fucking door before I kick it in!" Seven screamed.

Bryce walked over to the desk and called the front desk. "Can you please send security up to room 824. There's an irate woman outside my door causing a disturbance."

"Yes sir, security is on their way," the desk clerk replied.

Before Bryce could even put the phone down, Seven started kicking the door with every ounce of her strength. "Bryce open this door! Now!"

When the elevator doors opened moments later, two security guards stepped out and ran toward the room.

"Ma'am, step away from the door," the taller security guard said in a stern voice.

"Open this damn door. My husband is behind there with some woman. I just want to talk to him," Seven replied.

"Ma'am, we're here to escort you out. You're causing a disturbance," the other security replied.

"I'm not going anywhere. You hear that, Bryce. I'll be right here when you get finished with your whore!" Seven yelled.

Suddenly, some of the other guests staying on the floor started coming out to see what the commotion was all about. Both security guards hurried over to Seven.

"You have to leave the hotel right now," the taller security guard said.

"If you touch me, I'm going to sue this fucking hotel!" Seven warned.

As Bryce continued to look out the peep hole, Jayda suddenly began rubbing up and down his back. She then dropped to her knees and took his limp penis into her mouth. When the guards finally grabbed Seven and forcefully walked her down the hallway, Bryce turned around.

"Hold up for one second," he said to Jayda.

Bryce ran over to the hotel window. He watched as Seven walked out the doors moments later pushing the security guards and cursing like a sailor in a bar. Bryce shook his head as she crossed the street then got in her car, but didn't bother to drive away.

"I'm not feeling taken care of. For three thousand dollars, I wasn't expecting this," Jayda said.

Bryce finally turned from the window. *Did she just say three thousand? Damn, Angelique wasn't kidding when she said she knew bitches with money. At this rate I'll have Darrell's money in no time.* "Don't worry you'll get your money's worth." Bryce rushed over and tackled Jayda onto the bed. He wasted no time removing all her clothes. "This will be an experience you'll never forget."

Seven sat outside in her car dialing Bryce's cell phone repeatedly even though each call went straight to voice mail. She stared at the front door of the hotel, burning a hole through each female guest that left, trying to recognize a woman who looked desperate enough to hire an escort.

"I'm not leaving until his ass comes out," she said getting comfortable.

When Bryce finally came out the bathroom and put on his clothes several hours later, he couldn't believe his eyes when he walked over to the window. Seven's car was still outside in the same spot. He glanced at the clock which read 4:08 a.m.

"I need to try and get out of here," he said to himself.

Bryce walked over, picked up his envelope off the nightstand, then kissed Jayda on her forehead. He laughed as she rolled over onto the other side of the bed in a deep comatose sleep.

"Until next time, beautiful."

Bryce caught the elevator down thinking of how he was going to handle Seven. He knew she was in rare form by now, and would surely cause a scene when she saw him. When he reached the lobby, Bryce took a couple deep breaths. He started his way toward the front door, then quickly changed his mind. Instead, he walked up to a girl at the front desk.

"Hey, how are you?" he spoke.

She looked at Bryce and smiled. "Hey, how are you?"

She probably thought he was about to kick some game, but that was the last thing on his mind.

"Umm…is there another way out of here besides the front door. I gotta be honest, my crazy baby momma is outside waiting for me, and I can't deal with it right now."

The girl's smile faded like she was no longer interested. "Yeah, there's an emergency exit door downstairs by the gym that only allows people out, not in."

"That's great. Thanks."

When Bryce made his way downstairs and out the door, his plan was to get far enough away before calling a cab.

By the time Jayda finally got up and checked out, it was almost eight. Once she finally emerged from the glass doors to wait for her car, Seven suddenly popped her head up and stared in Jayda's direction. Even though she was tired, her vision was still on point. Seven eyed the red Hermes bag on her arm.

"Ain't no bitch rocking a $9,000 Birkin bag and don't have money," Seven said out loud. "It's gotta be her." Deciding to approach the woman, Seven jumped out and raced over to the valet area of the hotel.

"Excuse me, were you with a guy named Bryce last night?" Seven shouted.

Jayda looked around and hoped Seven wasn't talking to her. "I'm sorry, what did you say?"

"I said, were you with a guy named Bryce last night?"

By that time, Jayda's white Porshe Panamera had pulled up. As she went to give the valet attendant a twenty dollar tip, Seven jumped into her face.

"Please don't ignore me," Seven advised. "I need to know if you were with my husband last night."

Jayda pushed Seven back. "I have no idea what you're talking about, but don't let the expensive shit fool you. I'll fuck you up." She knew Seven was the crazy woman banging on the door, so she had to protect herself.

"Ladies, calm down. This is not the place to discuss something as delicate as this," the valet attendant said getting between them.

Suddenly, Seven tried a different approach. "Hey, listen I apologize for getting in your face. I'm tired and upset, and that was wrong. I'm just really trying to find him and I was hoping you could help. Can you at least answer this…did Angelique set this whole thing up?"

When Jayda gave the valet guy a 'mind your business look' and he finally walked away, she looked back at Seven. "Yeah, she did. I paid good money to have fun and it was worth every dime. He left before I did, so maybe he's on his way home." Jayda walked toward her car. "I hope everything works out for you," she said hopping into the driver's seat.

"How much did he charge?" Seven asked.

"It was the best $3,000.00 I've spent in a long time!" Jayda shot back then pulled off at top speed.

Seven ran across the street barely avoiding being hit by passing car, and jumped into her car leaving burnt rubber strips. The thought of Angelique charging women $3,000.00 to be with Bryce and her not seeing any of that money made her blood boil. She'd had enough. *I'm going to kill that no good bitch and I know just the place to do it,* she thought.

Chapter **Twenty-Four**

Seven sped across town until her car pulled up in front of an office building on Perido Street. She avoided every single person who said she couldn't double park her car while making her way to the information board next to the elevator. She wanted to know exactly which floor Angelique's office was on. Seven rode the elevator to the fifth floor before barging through the double glass doors of Sloan, Covington & King.

"Can I help you?" the elderly white receptionist asked.

"What you can do is get that lying bitch Angelique out here so I can get to the bottom of her and my husband!" Seven smacked her hand on the marble counter.

The receptionist didn't know how to respond. She sat there with a speechless daze. "You want me to do what?"

"That's okay, I'll do it myself," Seven responded. "Angelique, Angelique, where are you? I know you're in here you fucking whore! Show your face so I can show you what happens to bitches that fuck with other women's husbands!" she yelled.

As the receptionist quickly dialed for security, the office doors quickly began opening one by one. Seven continued to walk around the office screaming at the top of her lungs before Angelique finally snatched her door open.

"Seven, have you lost your mind? This is my place of business," Angelique said, walking toward her.

"Your place of business, that's funny. I thought your

business was pimping my husband out to your slutty friends for three grand. Don't try to deny it. I caught one of your hoe's with Bryce and she told me everything," Seven responded.

Angelique couldn't wait to call and curse Jayda out. She glanced at her co-workers who looked on in disbelief. "I think you're confused. Why don't you calm down and come into my office so we can straighten this out?"

"Bitch, I'm here to find out where you've hidden my husband, and I'm going to get the truth out of you one way or another. Even if I have to beat it out of you," Seven said walking closer to Angelique.

"Is there a problem?" Mr. Covington asked walking down the hall.

Now Angelique was nervous. "Oh no sir, there's no problem at all. I think this woman has me mixed up with someone else. I'll take care of this right away," Angelique answered. "Ms. Whitney, can you call security to see this woman out?" Angelique yelled.

"I've been calling but no one is answering the extension!" Ms. Whitney yelled back. "I'll keep trying!"

"I'm not going anywhere until I find out where Bryce is. I don't give a damn who you call," Seven said getting even closer.

Mr. Covington stepped in front of Seven's path. "Ma'am, this is a billion dollar firm. I can't have fighting in our hallways. What will our clients think if news about a street brawl reached their ears? There must be something we can do to resolve this matter."

"There's only one thing that'll make this right. If that bitch tells me where my husband is and she gives me the money she made off of his golden dick," Seven responded.

Mr. Covington looked confused. "Excuse me?"

"You heard me. You got a no good dirty pimp working for you. I know she's hiding him somewhere and selling him to her friends. I just want my man back so we can work this shit out," Seven replied.

Mr. Covington looked back at Angelique. Before she could respond to his inquiring eyes, a couple of security guards burst into the firm doors.

"What seems to be the problem?" one of them asked.

"We have a trespasser who needs to be escorted out the building." Ms. Whitney pointed toward Seven.

The security didn't hesitate running up to Seven and attempting to grab her arm. "Excuse me Miss, I'm going to have to ask you to leave," the female guard said.

"I'm not going anywhere until I find out where my man is!" Seven shouted even louder.

By this time Mr. Sloan and Mr. King had emerged from their offices as well. They joined the others who were gathered around looking at the show.

"I'm going to ask you one more time. You can leave without incident or we can forcefully make you leave. It's your decision," the male guard said as they got closer to Seven.

"You better not put your hands on me. I'll leave when that bitch tells me what I want to know," Seven said taking a fighting stance.

"Ms. Whitney, you should go ahead and dial 911 and have this woman arrested. She must be high on something and this is only going to get worse!" Angelique advised.

"It's going to get a lot worse if you don't place those dead presidents in my hand," Seven fired back.

"I knew it. You don't give a damn about Bryce. All you're concerned with is the money. Get this woman out of here now!" Angelique ordered the security guards.

The two guards quickly walked closer to Seven. "Play time is over. It's time for you to leave."

Everyone in the firm watched as they grabbed Seven by both arms and began pulling her out. Seven put up a little resistance while trying to free her arms by kicking over anything within her reach.

"You'll be seeing me again real soon, bitch. I won't have anything to say to you next time. I'm going to let my fist do all the talking for me from now on!" Seven ranted.

Angelique wanted to go in a room and hide from the embarrassment as everyone stared at her like she was about to respond.

"Okay, show time is over. Please get back to work," Mr. Sloan said.

"Ms. Lyles, we would like to speak to you in the conference room," Mr. King said as the rest of the firm went back to their desks giggling like school kids.

"I need a moment to get myself together and I'll be right in," Angelique responded.

"No, right now Ms. Lyles," Mr. King demanded in a stern voice.

Angelique looked at the faces of each partner and gave them a little nod. She then followed them into the conference room. Angelique heard snickering as she closed the glass doors behind her from the other coworkers still in the hallway.

"Do you have anything to say about what just happened?" Mr. King questioned.

"I would like to apologize for that little scene. A friend of mine is going through a real bad situation with his wife and I was giving him a little assistance. This will never happen again," she replied.

"Is there any truth to what that woman was accusing you of? Are you hiding her husband and…what's that word she said…pimping him out to your friends for money?" Mr. Sloan added.

Angelique shook her head. "No, sir not at all. There's no value in anything she said."

"I really hope not because we wanted to acknowledge all your hard work that you did for us at our Houston location and now the New Orleans location by extending you a full partnership in this firm," Mr. Covington informed.

Angelique's face lit up. "I don't know what to say. I would be honored to become a partner in this prestigious firm."

"I wasn't finished," Mr. Covington said cutting off Angelique's acceptance speech.

"I'm sorry, by all means, go on," Angelique replied.

"As you just stated, we're one of the oldest and most sought after law firms in the country. It wouldn't look good to our clients or stakeholders if a partner in this firm was mixed up in some type of sex scandal involving prostitution and illegal money."

Angelique cut him off again. "I can promise you that you won't have to worry about that."

When Mr. Covington gave her another harsh look, Angelique quickly rubbed her fingers across her lips to imitate her zipping them shut.

"You're a very talented woman. I've never seen anyone have such a rapport with people like you do. You've brought in some major clients and they all seem to have a deep loyalty to you. This partnership is because of things like that. But before we continue further with securing your name along with the others in this room, I think we should allow a cleanup period to the end of the month for you to make sure your personal affairs are in order."

"I'm so overwhelmed that my hard work and dedication to this firm hasn't gone without notice. It has always been one of my goals to work myself to partner status from the first day I signed my contract ten years ago. I really don't know what to say other than thank you," Angelique said.

"I didn't hear anything about your personal life. Being a partner is a twenty-four/seven job and anything you do is a reflection on this firm," Mr. Sloan added.

"My personal life will not be a concern for anyone in this room or our stakeholders. I was just trying to help a friend make it through a rough time. I promise not to let my generosity damage this firm or me," Angelique said in a sincere tone.

"That's all I needed to hear," Mr. Covington said.

All three men walked over and held out their hands. "Congratulations partner."

"Thanks," she replied.

As soon as the meeting was over, Angelique rushed to her office and dialed Hypnotic's number. "Drop all your plans for tonight because I need you in on this one."

Seven hurried home to see if she could possibly catch Bryce packing more clothes. He hadn't taken that many with him, so she knew he would run out at some point. Screeching to a halt in front of her apartment, Seven parked the car, then jumped out. After bursting through the door, she ran around to each room, but found no evidence that Bryce had stopped by.

Feeling completely out of control, it wasn't long before she flipped out. Walking into the bathroom first, Seven sent the soap, toothpaste, lotion and all her make-up flying onto the floor with one sweep of her right arm. She then pulled down the shower curtain and ripped all the decorative towels off the rack before heading to her bedroom.

She went straight to the closet, and started throwing the rest of Bryce's clothes onto the floor. As tears streamed down her face, Seven battled with how she'd let her life turn out. She'd gone from a happy independent woman to someone depending on a man just to make ends meet. A man who had the audacity to leave her after she'd struggled with him for years. Seven continued to throw things all around the room until suddenly she had an epiphany. Once she wiped her tears, Seven reached back into the closet and pulled out a black Maxi dress before running to the bathroom to take a shower. Hopefully the new plan she had would finally get Bryce home for good.

When Seven entered the salon an hour later, Camille once again yelled at her for not coming in or calling. However, the scorned look on Seven's face instantly made Camille fall back.

"Hey, it's Mike Tyson!" Ce-Ce yelled out.

Two of the other stylists laughed as Seven stomped toward the back. Everyone probably thought she was going into the break room, but Seven headed straight to Camille's office. Knowing that Camille kept a bottle of Grey Goose stashed in her desk drawer, Seven quickly pulled the bottle out, twisted the cap, then took a nice sized shot to the head. The warm liquor had a little sting to it as it traveled down her throat.

After putting the bottle back in its place, she walked into the bathroom and splashed some water on her face. Seven stared at her reflection in the mirror. She silently gave herself a pep talk and headed back out into the salon.

"So, are you working today?" Camille asked.

Seven shook her head. "No, I just came to holler at Ce-Ce for a second."

Ce-Ce turned around with a pair of flat irons in her hand. "Me. What do you need to talk to me about? I haven't seen your husband either."

Once again the other stylists chuckled.

Seven walked over to her. "Can you be serious for a second?" When Ce-Ce rolled her eyes then nodded, Seven continued. "This a bit private. Let's walk over to the shampoo bowls."

"Girl, make it quick," Ce-Ce said wobbling behind Seven.

Once they reached the shampoo area, Seven stepped closer to her. "I need you to do me a favor."

"It depends on the favor," Cee-Cee replied.

"Don't think I'm crazy, but I need a little of your urine."

Cee-Cee looked at Seven like she'd lost her mind. "What? Why the hell do you want my piss?"

"Ssshhh," Seven said looking around the salon. "If I tell you this, you gotta promise to keep it a secret. I don't even want Camille to know."

Ce-Ce immediately thought Seven wanted it for some type of drug test. "I promise."

At that moment, Seven went in her purse and pulled out a CVS bag. When Ce-Ce looked inside, there were two EPT tests along with a hundred dollar bill.

"I need you pee on those little sticks so I can confirm to

Bryce that I'm pregnant. I just need to get him home and away from that bitch. I need to remind his ass that I'm the best thing that ever happened to him," Seven uttered. "Making a hundred dollars just for some piss isn't a bad deal to me. Plus I know you could use it for damn pampers or something."

"So, why do you have two tests?" Cee-Cee asked.

"Bryce is a stickler for details. I need to have both of them with the plus sign to make sure he believes me."

Ce-Ce let out a long sigh. "Alright Seven, but don't ever ask me to do no shit like this again." Shaking her head, she headed to the bathroom in the back.

As Seven waited for Ce-Ce to return, her cell phone started to ring. Praying that it was Bryce, she sucked her teeth when she saw Stephon's name pop up.

"Oh, so you finally decided to call me back, huh?"

"I've been busy," he said with an attitude.

"Yeah, I heard. Busy shooting up garages."

Stephon got quiet for a minute. "Don't be sayin' no stupid shit like that over the phone. I didn't shoot up a damn thing."

"Umm hmm. Look, I need you to help me out with something."

"You know, Seven, I'm still pissed that you would play me like that in front of your punk ass husband that day," Stephon responded.

"Well, what the fuck did you expect me to do?"

"Tell him the truth so I wouldn't be standin' there lookin' dumb as a muthafucka. Tell 'em that you begged me to come ova your house and jerk off in front of you so you could show the video to your clients. Tell 'em how you agree to fuck me every time I give you money."

Seven chuckled. "Do you really think I was gonna admit that shit to my husband? I had to look out for my marriage."

"Yeah, okay and I recently had to look out for me."

Seven knew that was Stephon's way of admitting to the shooting. "So, are you gonna help me out or not?"

"Yeah, I guess. Even though I'm fucked up with you right now, I would never leave you hangin'," he said after a long pause.

"Good. I'll call you later with the details."

Seven hung up, but quickly called Bryce's number a few seconds later. As usual it went to voice mail, but this time instead of saying something nasty, she turned on the charm.

"Hey Bryce. Look, I'm not calling to harass you this time. I just want you to know that I'm sorry about everything, and that I don't blame you if you don't wanna come back. I'm not gonna bother you anymore. I just want you to know that I decided not to keep the baby. I just don't want to go through this alone. Talk to you soon…hopefully."

CLICK.

Chapter Twenty-Five

While Bryce sat on the couch eating a bowl of cereal, a text came through on his phone.

Sorry 4 the late notice, but I found a client willing to come to the apartment. She'll be there in 1 hour. Make sure you put it on her. LOL. I'll call u later.

XOXOX,

Angelique

Looking down at the time on his phone, it was after nine p.m. and after being out all day Bryce was beyond tired. He really wasn't in the mood to entertain, but Bryce knew he had to find the energy from somewhere in order to make the three grand. Looking back down at his phone, this time Bryce realized that he had several voice messages. Majority of the time they were from Seven, and lately he'd been listening to them strictly for entertainment. He leaned back against the cushion as Seven's messages played one after the other. But it was the message about her going to terminate the pregnancy that he actually replayed before deciding to return her call. He slowly dialed Seven's number.

"Hello," she whispered into the phone.

"Hey, what's up?"

Seven smiled. She knew he would call once she threatened to kill their make believe child. "Nothing much."

"I heard your message. So, are you sure that's what you wanna do because if so, I wouldn't agree."

"Why not, Bryce? It's obvious that you're not coming back, so why would I raise a child on my own. You know about my childhood. I don't want my baby being raised without a father."

"Don't act like I left because of something I did," Bryce responded.

"Look, I understand that you were upset to find Stephon in our shower, but you over reacted. I wasn't naked. We weren't fucking. I was working on getting us money to reach our goals of building a life together," Seven tried to explain.

"So, I'm supposed to believe that you did that for us? Just like you wanted me to believe that you were just a stripper. Just like you wanted me to believe that he was your brother."

"It's the truth, but I'm not going to apologize for something I didn't do. And I'm definitely not raising a child on my own."

"No one said you had to," Bryce shot back.

"Okay, I hear you, and if I made the mistake of expanding the business without you knowing then I apologize for that. My intention was to share the video with you when you got home, but obviously I never got the chance."

Bryce rubbed his head. "What else haven't you shared with me?"

"What else haven't I shared? Ain't that the kettle calling the pot black? What haven't you shared? I heard your phone ringing in that hotel room, and I could hear you talking. You wouldn't even open the door, so that's pretty fucked up. Plus, I heard you're working for Angelique now for three grand a date, so if you wanna blame someone for being deceitful then you better point at yourself," Seven answered.

"I just can't trust you, Seven," Bryce said.

"Well, don't trust that bitch Angelique either. Her fake next top model ass is pretending to be a savior on a white horse when she ain't nothing but a jealous bitch wanting what's mine."

"Are you referring to me or the money?" Bryce quickly responded.

"Are you serious? My money is your money and that's always been the case. Whatever money was made went to better us. I'm the future mother of your child and I deserve much more than this blatant disrespect."

Bryce was quiet for a moment. "This conversation is too much. I gotta go."

"What? You're going to get off with me, just like that. Did Angelique tell you that it was time to go?" Seven yelled.

"No, she didn't."

Before Seven could get another word in, the line went dead. Bryce didn't want to be mentally drained before his client got there, so he turned off his cell, then went to freshen up. By the time the woman knocked on the door forty-five minutes later, Bryce had the lights dim, candles burning and Maxwell's *Urban Hang Suite* CD playing in the background.

Spraying some of his cologne into the air, Bryce put the bottle on the dining room table before answering the door. He was surprised to see Hypnotic.

"Hey sexy," she said inviting herself in.

Bryce closed the door. "Hey…I didn't know you were the client."

"Yep. After what Angelique told me about you, there was no way I was gonna miss out on this."

"So, she doesn't mind if we…you know," Bryce stated.

"Not at all. My cousin isn't selfish. She doesn't mind sharing." Hypnotic threw her Artsy Louis Vuitton bag on the couch. "So, it's no sense in wasting time. Let's get started in the bedroom."

Well, a job is a job, Bryce thought as he immediately starting performing a little strip tease for her. Since Hypnotic was in the business he knew she could appreciate a good show. Hypnotic became horny as Bryce wiggled his ripped body in front of her. Once he pulled down his boxers and showed a fully erect dick, her eyes widened.

Bryce pulled Hypnotic into his arms and carried her into the bedroom. He slowly removed her tight embellished dress as they kissed passionately. He wasn't surprised that she wasn't wearing any panties. Bryce softly placed Hypnotic on the bed, crawled on top of her and then proceeded to have the most incredible sex that she'd ever experienced.

Hour after hour Hypnotic moaned louder with each passing orgasm. She laughed then cried until her body was completely exhausted. Once their night was complete, Bryce left her lying in the bed snoring as if she'd worked a double shift at some factory. Bryce stood in the bathroom letting the shower water get to the perfect temperature, when suddenly he heard voices coming from the bedroom. Trying to eavesdrop, he quietly cracked the door open to see who Hypnotic was talking to.

"Girl, he was everything you said and even more. My pussy won't feel the same for days," Hypnotic said.

"I told you. Wait…does your dumb ass have me on speaker? Take me off," Angelique huffed.

"Chill out, Cuz. He's in the shower. I acted like I was sleep when he got up, so it's all good. Besides, I'm too fucking worn out to hold the phone," Hypnotic replied with a slight laugh. "So, did you remember to set up the camcorder?"

"Yeah, while he was out today I came in and put it in the closet. I made sure it was facing the bed. Please tell me that the closet door wasn't closed when you walked into the room."

"No, it wasn't."

"Good, make sure you get it before he gets out."

Bryce could hear Hypnotic moving around. "Let me get it now. Are you sure the camera got everything if you planted it hours ago?"

"It should've. The camera records up to fifteen hours," Angelique informed. "Wait until Seven gets a hold of this video. That bitch will really be enraged once she sees you fucking her man. This is just step one though. Step two will be when he falls in love with me and divorces her ass. It'll be the ultimate payback."

"So, if you think he's starting to have feelings for you are those feelings mutual? Do you like him, too?'

"Trust me, he can definitely fuck, and I do think he's a nice guy. But I could never be with a man like Bryce. I need someone who's more on my level…intellectually and financially. He's beneath me. I mean how much is that garage he wants gonna make? He couldn't afford me," Angelique bragged.

"Well, if he keeps going out on dates with all your friends then he'll start making good money then. We're going to get Seven, but I think we need to clean his ass out, too," Hypnotic replied.

"It wasn't even about the money at first, but I guess you're right. Maybe I do need to take a cut," Angelique responded. "Might as well make some cash before I dismiss him."

"Well, I'm gonna leave the money for this date like you said, but I'ma need my shit back at some point," Hypnotic warned.

Angelique laughed. "I got you."

When Bryce turned off the water like he was getting out, Hypnotic quickly told Angelique she had to go. He didn't say two words to her as Hypnotic grabbed her belongings and hurried out the door. He was still in shock that Angelique had betrayed him and didn't waste any time thinking of ways to deal with the situation.

BEDROOM GANGSTA

Chapter Twenty-Six

Bryce kept in contact with Angelique over the next two days but only through text. He needed time to get his head together as the conversation between her and Hypnotic constantly consumed his thoughts. However, with the two week deadline steadily approaching, Bryce had to put together a plan that would guarantee him money while seeking revenge at the same time. Once he came up with the perfect solution, Bryce sent Angelique a text stating that he needed to speak with her face to face.

I can stop by 2nite. Hey, I know u needed some time 2 yourself, but I have several dates lined up, she replied.

That's what I wanted to talk about. Time is running out so I need to go on several dates. At least four. Plus I wanna talk to u about something really important, Bryce replied.

No problem. I have 2 ladies who've signed up. By the time I get there I'll have 2 more. See u tonight around nine.

Wanting to be well rested when she arrived, Bryce took a nap for almost four hours until a knock on the door pulled him out of his slumber. He jumped up out of the bed, hurried to the door and peeked through the peep hole. A smile crept over his face as he opened the door.

"I'm glad to see that you got my text," Bryce said.

"You know I got your back."

"You can go set up in the bedroom. Angelique should be here any minute," Bryce instructed.

"Okay."

Just like clockwork Angelique slid her key through the door at exactly nine p.m. Bryce hated that she had complete access to his temporary home, but couldn't complain when the apartment belonged to her in the first place.

When Angelique stepped into the apartment, Bryce raced into her arms and kissed her with a tremendous explosion of passion.

"Wow! If I didn't know better, I would think that you really missed me," Angelique said when Bryce finally pulled his tongue from her mouth.

"I've missed you more than words can express. You've been my every thought."

"Whatever, I'm here so what's the big emergency?" she asked.

"Well, I've been giving it some major thought. I feel that you and I are just perfect for each other. I've filed divorce papers and I'm hoping that you'll give this relationship a chance," Bryce said, grabbing both of Angelique's hands.

Angelique looked surprised. She couldn't believe that her plan had worked so soon. "Are you serious? I don't think Seven is gonna go away that fast. I never told you that her crazy ass came to my job the other day and caused a major scene. We had to call security."

"Really?"

"Yeah, the senior partners have given me thirty days to prove to them that my personal life is in order before I make partner because of that shit," Angelique informed.

Bryce yanked Angelique into a hard embrace. He then leaned in and kissed her with even more passion. "Well, you don't have to worry about her anymore. I'll definitely take care of Seven."

"That's good to know. I can't wait until we're rid of her," Angelique replied with excitement. "Now, let's discuss these dates."

"No…in the bedroom," Bryce said.

He lifted Angelique into his arms and carried her into the bedroom. He then gently placed her on the bed. Bryce removed her shoes, massaging each foot. He slid his tongue up her legs as his fingers slowly unfastened the buttons on her dress.

"I've written down four women's names and contact information. Even though I've already talked to them about the dates, I still wanted you to be able to call them just in case something comes up on your end."

"Sounds good to me, but is it possible for me to do three dates tomorrow. I really need to get this done."

"Damn, that's a lot, but I'll switch some things around. I was thinking that since I've been working so hard that I could get a portion of the money from the dates this time. That's if you don't mind," Angelique responded.

Bryce reflected back on her and Hypnotic's conversation and smiled. "I don't mind at all. Now, let's get back to business."

He placed different parts of her body into his mouth while his hands tossed her outfit across the room. Angelique closed her eyes to take pleasure in the indescribable feelings that Bryce had running up and down her body. Bryce took his time removing her lace bra and thong. He then opened her legs and pressed his face against her dripping pussy. He flicked his tongue against her clit until her body began to shake.

Angelique rubbed Bryce's head holding him in certain spots until she squirted cum all over his face. Bryce pinched her hardened nipples as he drove his tongue further into her overflowing paradise. Her moans continued to increase in volume as his tongue banged against her walls. Seconds later, Bryce made his way up her body, caressing her breast and licking her neck. He paused long enough to crawl off of Angelique and remove all his clothes.

"Turn off the lights," Angelique said, kicking all the covers off of the bed.

"I want the lights on. I love to see your facial expressions when you cum," Bryce replied sliding back on top of her.

After ninety minutes of non-stop fucking, Angelique needed a bathroom break. She kissed the tip of Bryce's dick as she got up off the bed. Bryce smacked her ass and watched her every step until she disappeared behind the bathroom door. Suddenly, a figure raced out of the open closet without saying a word and dashed past him. Bryce could only smile. Moments later, Angelique stepped out of the bathroom ready to begin another session. The sound of a front door being shut caught her attention.

"What was that?" she asked.

"What was what?"

"I think I heard something in the other room. Maybe it was the front door. It may be somebody knocking. You're not expecting a client are you?"

Bryce got up. "I'll go check but I didn't hear anything." Bryce laughed as he got to the door and pretended to be looking for someone. "Nope, you must be hearing things." he added when he returned to the bedroom.

Angelique crawled onto the bed and got into the doggy style position. "Okay, I hope you're ready because you have more to do."

Bryce smiled as he thought about how he'd used Angelique's own plan in order to get his payback.

Hypnotic couldn't be more excited as she danced around the house with her third glass of wine. Not only was she still in a good mood from the experience she'd had with Bryce, but she was also ready to mail their home made porno out to Seven. Because she'd been so busy Hypnotic hadn't even watched the video herself. She looked around the house for a while, but after realizing that she'd left it in her car, Hypnotic grabbed her robe and headed outside. Hypnotic didn't live in a bad neighborhood, so she left the door cracked which is something she did all the time.

"I wish I could see Seven's face when she looks at this shit," Hypnotic said to herself as she opened her car door and retrieved the DVD.

After walking back into her house, she headed for the kitchen. Hypnotic poured herself another glass of wine then made her way to the bedroom where she kept the DVD player. She couldn't wait to view the footage. However, before she even made an attempt to turn on her T.V., suddenly her bedroom door slammed shut.

Hypnotic turned around to find a man with a ski mask and dressed in all black standing directly behind her. What made things even worse was the six inch knife in the man's right hand. Terrified, Hypnotic screamed to the top of her lungs then threw her glass before making a mad dash for the bathroom. But he managed to leap over the bed and catch her. He threw her against the back wall, knocking over the lamp in the corner.

"I'll slit your fuckin' throat if you make another sound," he said, throwing Hypnotic onto the floor.

Seconds later, he jumped on top of her, then covered her mouth with his gloved hand. Hypnotic tried to fight him off, but the perpetrator slammed her head against the floor a couple of times sending a ringing sound directly through her ears.

"You can fight back all you want. That'll only make this more enjoyable. Now, nod your fuckin' head if you understand." He placed the knife against her throat with his free hand.

Hypnotic slowly shook her head up and down. She watched as the knife left her throat then traveled down to her torso. Tears streamed down her face as her robe, wife beater and pink panties were cut open by the long blade. Moments later she felt the man pulling down his pants and inserting his dick into her dry pussy. Hypnotic wanted to scream out in pain, but bit her lip to hold it in.

The attacker continued to ram his dick further inside as

her tears rushed down her face like a waterfall. His muscular frame pounded harder with each thrust before his body finally indicated that an orgasm was near. When she finally felt the man's body jerk, Hypnotic used that perfect opportunity to reach up and knock the knife out of his hand. They instantly began tussling on the floor until she was able to grab his head. Hypnotic refused to let go while he desperately tried to remove her hands. With one last tug she pulled the mask off revealing her attacker.

With his face exposed, Stephon panicked. He quickly crawled over and punched her in the face. He then wrapped both his hands around her throat and squeezed with all his strength. Stephon continued to apply pressure until Hypnotic's body went completely limp.

Chapter **Twenty-Seven**

Seven almost burnt a hole in the floor as she paced the living room back and forth. She'd been waiting for Stephon's call since the night before and still hadn't heard from him. She was excited to hear about all the details including the look on Hypnotic's face when see saw Stephon in her house. Seven wasn't even sure how he'd gotten in, but hoped that the warning was good enough to let Hypnotic know that she wasn't to be fucked with. Seven stopped for a moment when she heard Moochie cursing somebody out next door.

"I can't wait to move out of this place," she said once Moochie kicked it up to second gear.

Seven was just about to bang on the wall when suddenly there was a knock on the door. Thinking it might've been Stephon, she quickly made her way to the door without bothering to see who it was. Seven couldn't stop smiling when Bryce handed her a dozen of pink and white tiger lilies.

"These are my favorite," she said, grabbing the vase.

"I know. I haven't been gone that long," Bryce replied with a huge smile. "So, are you gonna let me in?"

Seven stepped out of the way. "Of course. Why did you knock? You could've just used your key."

Bryce walked over toward the couch as Seven closed the door, then placed the flowers on the coffee table. "I wanted to be respectful."

"You look a little tired," she said.

"Yeah, I am. I've had a busy day. Just think, it's ten o'clock at night and I've already gone on two dates. I'm actually on my way to the third one, but wanted to stop by here first."

"Oh." Seven felt a bit jealous, but didn't want to ruin the moment.

"So, do you have it?" Bryce asked.

"Yeah, it's right here," Seven said walking over to re-trieve a disc from the counter. "It came out really well. I was pissed when you all first started fucking. The look on her face shows just how good you are. But once I thought about the rea-son why you asked me to come over and tape it, that's the only thing that calmed me down."

"This plan has to work," Bryce replied.

"Why did you ask me anyway? You could've easily asked Mitch to do it."

"Well, I just figured that you would love to get back at Angelique like me."

"I tried to tell you that the bitch was foul."

"And I should've listened. Now it's time to put the sec-ond part into action. Do you know what to do with the disc?" Bryce questioned.

"I need you to walk me through it one more time."

"On this paper is a list of partners in Angelique's firm along with their email addresses. I also went on the firm's web-site and got several other associates email addresses so it would-n't hurt to send it to them, too. Shit, send it to Angelique as well. She's up for a partnership, but its contingent on her not doing anything to embarrass the firm. If you email this to everyone on that list, she won't be getting a partnership or anything else for that matter."

"I like it. This will teach her to fuck with another woman's husband," Seven said.

"You might as well wait until the morning though. That way everyone will be in the office," Bryce replied. "Okay one last thing…"

Just as Bryce was about to explain he glanced over to the T.V. and saw Hypnotic's picture displayed on Fox's ten o'clock nightly news. He quickly told Seven to hand him the remote so he could turn it up.

"We're recapping this story about an African American woman brutally raped and murdered last night in the Old Aurora neighborhood. The woman, who was identified as twenty-nine year old Crystal Reynolds was apparently strangled to death in her home. Police tell us as of right now there are no known suspects. However, there was a black ski mask left behind on the scene, which police are positive was used in the crime."

As a composite of the mask was shown on the screen, Seven felt like she was about to throw up. Even Bryce was disturbed. He was pissed that Hypnotic was involved in Angelique's little scheme, but never wished any physical harm to her.

"Damn, that's fucked up. I feel bad. Who would do something like that?" he asked.

"I have no idea," Seven spoke in a low tone.

"You better make sure this door is locked at night. People are crazy out here."

Seven nodded her head. "I see."

Bryce was silent for a moment, before looking at the time on the cable box. "I need to get out of here. What I was trying to say before all this is that I don't wanna take my money to the next date. Could I leave it here with you?"

"Yeah…sure."

"I trust you more than I trust my date. You never know, bitches rob too these days."

Seven let out a smile as she followed Bryce into the bedroom. Luckily, she'd cleaned up after her small tirade a few days ago, so he wouldn't think she was crazy. Grabbing an empty Nike boot box, Bryce placed several bundles of cash inside. A small devilish grin came over her face as Bryce closed the lid, then placed the box in the back of the closet.

"It's thirty thousand in there. I finally have more than enough for my garage, so tonight will be my last escort," Bryce informed.

"Damn, you must've fucked a ton of bitches to get that type of money," Seven joked. "But I'm happy for you though," Seven replied.

"I'm gonna be too tired to come back tonight and get it, so I'll come back tomorrow. Is that okay?"

"Yeah, that's perfectly fine." For once she wasn't even concerned about him staying.

Bryce stepped up to his wife. "Everything is going to work out. Soon, this escort thing will be a distant memory and we'll be living the life that was always meant for us."

"I have no worries that everything will work out," Seven replied. "As a matter of fact, let me show you something." She walked over to her purse and pulled out both of the EPT tests. "I just wanted to show you these just in case you thought I was lying."

Bryce displayed a huge smile. "Wow, so you really are pregnant. Are you still considering getting rid of the baby though?"

"I don't think so."

"I love you," Bryce said before giving her a soft kiss on her lips.

Seven hadn't heard those three words in a long time. "I love you, too."

As soon as Bryce headed out the door, Seven grabbed her phone and quickly dialed Stephon's number. When he didn't answer, she hung up and called right back. When it got to the forth ring, this time he picked up.

"Hello."

"Stephon, what did you do?"

"I don't wanna talk over the phone. I'll be over there in a minute," Stephon responded.

"No, I don't want you over here until you tell me what happened."

"I went over there like you told me, but shit got out of hand. She pulled my fuckin' mask off, so I had to…you know."

"But that wasn't what I sent you to do. You were just supposed to scare her. You'll have to deal with that outcome on your own. I can't help you on this one."

"You won't have to. When we met up about the plan over your house, I took one of Bryce's old garage jumpsuits when you used the bathroom. See, I needed some insurance just in case this got ugly, so I planted that shit in her house. I'm sure the police will probably be looking for Bryce at some point…not me. Once they catch him then we can be together."

Seven went silent. She was pissed at Bryce for several reasons, but wasn't going to send him to jail for something he didn't do. "You also left your ski mask idiot."

"So what. How is that shit gonna prove I did it?" Stephon asked. "Besides, why the fuck do you wanna keep talkin' about this shit over the phone? Seven, don't fuck with me. I love you and all, but trust me…I'm not goin' to jail behind this."

At that moment, Seven knew her life would ultimately be in danger at some point. "Calm down. I'm just asking. Look, I'll call you back when I figure this shit out," she said hanging up.

Over the next several minutes Seven ran around the house grabbing all the things she needed. Tomorrow was going to be a big day for her with several things on the agenda, one which included the New Orleans Police Department.

Chapter Twenty-Eight

The next day, Seven walked out of the police station with a weight lifted off of her shoulders. Once Stephon threatened her in his usual incognito type of way, she knew he was better off locked behind bars as opposed to being out on the street. After informing detectives that she knew something about the woman being murdered in Old Aurora, Seven made up a story about overhearing Stephon confess to the rape and murder while at a friend's house. She then proceeded to give them his address and anything else they needed. Seven knew that once they finally locked Stephon up, it would be a substantial evidence case. However, once they tested his semen for DNA, that proof would surely be the nail in his coffin.

When Seven left the station, she drove straight over to the salon where she double parked out front. She switched her body through the front door carrying nothing but a small plastic bag. Seven didn't speak to anyone. She just walked to the empty styling station where she kept a few of her belongings, then started putting them into the bag.

"What's going on, Seven?" Camille asked.

"I've decided to finally leave this dump," Seven said without looking up.

Camille's big eyes bulged. "Dump, my shop ain't a dump. You know what, I've had enough of your ass. After all

I've tried to do for you, you wanna come in here out the blue and talk shit. I should've fired you a long time ago. That's right, get your stuff. It ain't nothing but two smocks and a pair of raggedy ass tennis shoes anyway. Don't nobody want that shit," Camille fired back. She didn't care about her client etiquette at that point.

"This a prime example of why hood chicks will never have a respectful business," Seven said, shaking her head.

As Camille walked over to Seven, Cee Cee quickly blocked her. "Girl, she ain't worth it. She's a lottery hoe looking for the next quick payday."

"Fuck you, too Cee Cee. Don't expect me to be your bastard child's Godmother now," Seven responded.

"Get the fuck out my shop!" Camille shouted.

"You don't have to ask me twice. I was so much better than this place when I first walked through the door," Seven said grabbing the bag.

"You reap what you sow!" Camille yelled just as Seven walked out of the front door.

After throwing the bag in the front seat, Seven sped over to Starbucks a few blocks from the salon and parked her car. Grabbing her laptop, she quickly went inside and ordered a China Greentips tea before finding a seat near the front window. Once she was settled, Seven took a few sips of her tea while waiting for her laptop to boot. A few minutes later, she clicked on the wireless internet button, then headed straight to Gmail where she'd already set up a fake account.

As soon as she logged in, Seven pulled out the paper with all the emails that Bryce had written down and started typing. Next she put in large capitalized letters the words BE CAREFUL WHO YOU HIRE...LAWYER GONE WILD in the subject line.

Attached to this email is proof that your associate, Angelique Lyles, is deeply involved in illegal prostitution. This is what a female pimp looks like in action. What values does your firm believe in to employ such a person?

Seven laughed as she loaded the disc into her computer, then attached the file. All she needed to do now was hit send. Seven grabbed her phone and called Angelique's firm.

"Ms. Lyles' office. How may I assist you?" Regina answered.

"I would like to speak with Ms Lyles. This is *Mrs.* Deans," Seven replied.

"I'm sorry but Ms. Lyles is not in right now. She's out due to a family death. Would you like to?" Regina stopped in mid sentence. "Wait a minute Ms. Lyles is walking in right now." Regina paused for a brief moment. "Ms. Lyles, I have a Mrs. Deans on the line. Would you like to speak to her?"

"The name Mrs. Deans doesn't sound familiar, but okay," Angelique replied.

"One moment, Ma'am," Regina said, placing Seven on hold.

Seven must've waited for nearly five minutes before Angelique finally came on the line.

"This is Ms. Lyles." It sounded like she'd just got finished crying.

"Does the name Mrs. Deans sound familiar to you now," Seven asked.

"Look, I'm really not in the mood to deal with any bullshit today. Do you know that Hypnotic is dead?" Angelique's voice cracked.

"Yeah, I heard, but that's not why I'm calling. I thought I'd give you the heads up that today will be the worse day of your life," Seven replied.

"Look, stop harassing me. I just lost my cousin. It's not my fault that Bryce doesn't want you anymore."

"Say what you want. That's why I have a video tape of you and Bryce fucking and talking about setting up escorts. You and your dumb cousin shouldn't have been talking so loud about destroying me and fucking him over. He heard the whole plan. That's how Bryce came up with the video stunt. He also gave me a list of all the people in your firm with their email addresses. I'm about to send your nasty bedroom practices to all your coworkers," Seven answered.

Angelique's eyes widened. "What? I don't believe you."

"You don't have to wait long. As a matter of fact, I'm about to hit the send button right now. Let's see if you still get that promotion when everyone sees you bent up like a pretzel with a married man talking about escorting."

Angelique paused. "Wait…please. I'll pay you not to send that email. How much money do you want?"

"A million dollars," Seven answered.

"What…are you crazy? I don't have that type of money."

"Well, that was my only price. I guess it's time to get started on that worse day of your life," Seven said hanging up. Within seconds the email was sent.

As several tears rushed down Angelique's face, the sound of her email notification came through. Glancing at the computer, as soon as she saw the subject from Seven's email, Angelique didn't even bother to open it up. Instead she gathered her purse along with her law degree off the wall and several photos before walking out of her office. By the time she made it to the corner, several gasps from her co-workers began to ring out from every cubicle and office. Her eyes were burning by the time she left out of the firm's doors. Angelique didn't even wait for the elevator. She ducked into the stairway then began walking down as her heels echoed with each step.

When Bryce emerged from Houston's, he heard his cell phone ringing, but his hands were so full with lunch for him and Seven, he didn't have a chance to answer. By the time he made it to the car his phone was ringing again.

"Hello," Bryce said putting the bags down.

"How could you? I thought you cared about me," Angelique cried into the phone.

"What are you talking about?"

"Are you serious? You're going to act like you don't know what I'm talking about. Your wife emailed me and every-one at my job a video of us fucking."

Bryce didn't respond.

"How could you do this to me after all I did for you?" Angelique belted.

"You should've thought about that shit before you ran your mouth to your cousin about me being beneath you. Saying that I wasn't your type and that this whole thing was just to get back at Seven. I was really starting to care about you."

"Who told you those lies? I never said anything like that. I really do have feelings for you. I only wanted Hypnotic to be-lieve that I didn't. I fell in love with you. At least, I did before you could bring yourself to do something like this to me."

"You're lying, Angelique. Don't you get it? I heard you and Hypnotic's conversation that night. The night you called her over so she could fuck me. The night you planted a camera in the closet."

Angelique was caught, so it was no need to try and de-fend herself anymore. "I can't believe you fucked up my life for a woman who doesn't give a damn about you."

"Shut up. You don't know shit about me and Seven's re-lationship."

"Oh yeah, well I know that once I call all those women and make up a few lies you're gonna be done in this business. You'll never get that fucking garage."

"Actually I will. You must've forgotten that I went on my forth date early this morning, so now I have more than enough cash to give Darrell his twenty-percent. Consider me out of the business now."

Bryce could hear Angelique sobbing in the phone, but he didn't have any remorse. "Stop worrying about me and Seven now anyway. What you need to be worried about is finding a new job," he said hanging up.

Bryce's phone kept ringing, but he didn't answer. He looked possessed to other motorist as he laughed hysterically driving down the street thinking of Angelique's cries. When he pulled up in front of his apartment a few minutes later Seven's car wasn't outside.

Maybe she finally decided to go to work today, he thought.

Deciding to take the food in the house anyway, Bryce grabbed the bag, then hopped out of the car. After making his way inside, he hadn't even made it past the living room when he saw the Nike box that contained his money on the floor. Looking at the upside down box could only mean one thing…it was empty. Instantly dropping the food, Bryce picked up the box, then threw it across the room.

"That bitch!"

He quickly dialed Seven's number. When she didn't answer Bryce scurried out the apartment, jumped down sets of steps and raced down the street. Bryce took out his phone and dialed her number again. This time Seven answered.

"Hello, my dear," she said in a very pleasant voice.

"I'm really disappointed in you."

"And why would you say that?"

"Where the fuck is my money?"

"I didn't leave you a thank you note. Oh, I'm sorry. Your money is right here with me like it should be," Seven answered. "Did you really think I would want your ass after you fucked all those women? If so, you've got to be the dumbest nigga alive. I can't believe that I saw anything in you. I take that back. I saw dollar signs in your ass and that's just what I got. This thirty grand is a nice little nest egg for me to start some type of business," Seven said laughing.

Bryce laughed even harder. "Hey Seven, when did a crack baby like you think you were smarter than me?"

"What?" Seven screamed.

"How much money did you really get from me? Do you have any idea? Did you even look at the money? I bet you just dumped all the shit in a bag without even looking at it, huh? You're such a rookie thief. Or like a said before a money-hungry bitch."

"Don't be mad because I played you. I made you go out and sell your body and then took all the money and now I'm leaving you with nothing."

"Like I said, when did you think you were smarter than me? Why don't you see just how much you made off with? I bet you'll be surprised."

Seven thought about it for a moment. She pulled her car over, grabbed the back pack from the front seat and unzipped it. Pulling out a bundle of money, she quickly yanked the rubber band off. Seven's eyes increased as she looked at the stack that only had one real ten dollar bill on top. The rest was fake play money that could be found in any party store. She couldn't believe it. Seven pulled out wad after wad and had the same outcome.

"So, let's see…thirty bundles times ten dollars…what's that three hundred dollars. Wow you really made out with a lot," Bryce laughed. "Who's the dumb bitch now?"

"You're a no good bastard!" Seven shouted.

"Oh, and that's not all. Did your dumb ass forget that Reggie from the garage was Cee Cee's boyfriend? He called me the day you asked Cee Cee to piss on those EPT tests. It never ceases to amaze me how low you'll stoop to get what you want. Look for the divorce papers in the mail. Have a nice fucking life."

CLICK.

Epilogue

Six Months Later

Angelique sat in her silver Honda Accord trade-in listening to the two-way portable radio mounted on her dashboard. She opened up the newspaper and searched for the ad that she'd bought to be placed in the Alabama Gazette. The Tuscaloosa weather forecast called for another beautiful spring day in the mid 80's, but Angelique had all four of her windows down instead of running the AC. These days it was all about saving. The days of spending unnecessarily were over since she wasn't making nearly as much as she used to. After losing her job and being black balled by the firm, Angelique moved two hundred and ninety miles away to try and obtain a new life. But instead of representing some athlete with a multi million dollar contract, now she was representing accident victims.

On top of that New Orleans just reminded her so much of Hypnotic, who she thought about almost every second of the day. She was overjoyed when they arrested her killer, but that still didn't heal the wound in her heart. She shook her head once she found her ad in disbelief that she was now chasing ambulances just to make ends meet. She couldn't believe how fast her life had taken a turn for the worst. But nowadays it was all about creating a fresh start and trying to rebuild from the ground up. She tried hard to forget that past hurtful section of her life, vowing never to return.

"Ambulance 3846, we have a call of an accident in front of Food World Grocery. 641 Bear Creek Road. Possible injuries!" an operator blasted over the radio.

Knowing that was her cue, Angelique started up her car and pulled out of the Mini-Mart parking lot. She raced through traffic trying to be the first lawyer on site. When Angelique arrived only ten minutes later, she parked her car in the middle of the next block so no one would see her getting out. She then opened her door, tossed her purse over her shoulder and marched up to the scene.

Angelique surveyed the area looking for all injured parties. *Time to make that money*, she thought as a policeman began putting up yellow tape to block off on-lookers. Angelique walked over and held out her card.

"I'm sorry, you can't go any further," the officer said rejecting the card.

"You don't understand, I have a client over there that needs their attorney. I would hate to include you in the law suit because you kept me from assisting them," Angelique replied in a stern voice. She may not have been a top sports attorney anymore, but was still good at talking shit.

The policeman paused for a second. He looked Angelique up and down. After a moment of deliberation, he lifted the tape to allow Angelique access to the scene. She immediately went to the three women sitting on the curb and instructed them not to speak to anyone else other than her.

As Seven walked toward the doors of the strip club with a cute round belly, the bouncers couldn't believe their eyes.

"Damn, who was able to tie you down long enough to knock your ass up," Niko joked. When the other bouncer laughed, Seven rolled her eyes and moved both men out of her way. "Who are you here to see Seven? Ain't no way Speedy gonna put you on stage in that condition," Niko added.

As Seven continued into the club, she thought to herself how Speedy definitely wasn't the person she was there to see. It was Mitch. He'd missed two payments in a row, and she desperately needed some cash. Working part time at Forever 21 didn't satisfy all the money she paid out in bills every month, so she looked forward to Mitch's stipend every week.

As Seven looked around but didn't see Mitch behind any of the bars she rubbed her twenty-six week stomach. It still even surprised her how she'd decided to keep the baby once she found out that she really was pregnant. What was more surprising was when she did the math and realized that Stephon was the father. She couldn't remember the last time Bryce had cum inside of her, and as many times she'd fucked Stephon for money there was no question who the baby belonged to. Instead of a hard working man who desperately tried to please his wife, her baby's father was a convicted life-sentence felon without parole. Someone she'd help put behind bars.

Every time Seven thought about Bryce and how good their marriage could've turned out if she hadn't been so malicious she became sad. She cursed herself for not being satisfied while they were together and forcing him to be with other women for the sake of money. Because Bryce filed for divorce under grounds of adultery, it only took four months for everything to be finalized. Now Seven was a single woman all because she didn't want to struggle. The punch line to this joke is that she struggled more now then she did when her and Bryce were together. Now Camille's 'you reap what you sow' final message was clearer than ever.

Seven walked over to the main bar, and slapped her hand on the counter to get the bartender's attention. "Where's Mitch?" she said when the bartender turned around.

"Who?"

"Don't play with me, Sam. Where's Mitch?"

"Damn, you haven't heard? Mitch is dead," Sam replied.

"You don't have to cover for him. This is not his baby,"

Seven said.

"I'm not kidding, Seven. Mitch killed himself about two weeks ago. I can't believe you didn't hear about that shit. He got caught on some camera at his construction job sucking some dude's dick. I heard the dudes on his job gave him some type of gay bashing beat down before his boss fired him. I even heard his boss threatened to put the video on Youtube. I guess it was too much for that nigga to handle so he took a whole bunch of prescription pills or something. I wondered why I didn't see you at the funeral."

Seven didn't know whether to laugh or cry. With Mitch as her last chance at making some easy money, she had no idea what to do next. As tears filled her eyes, Seven turned to leave, but bumped directly into Gwen, her old boss at the escort service. Gwen glanced down at Seven's belly poking out.

"I know you can't be working in your condition," Gwen stated.

"No, I was just looking for someone."

"Wow! I had no idea. When are you due?"

"In three months," Seven answered trying to hurry the conversation along.

"I'm happy for you. If there's anything I can do, don't hesitate to call me," Gwen replied. When she saw the desperate look on Seven's face, she held out her card. "I changed my number. Just give me a call. You know I have several clients who wouldn't mind you being pregnant."

Seven stared at Gwen then back at the card for what seemed like forever. "I'll call you tomorrow."

Bryce pulled up in front of the garage to find cars waiting in the parking lot. He noticed that several of the mechanics were already busy working and the neon OPEN sign was already lit in the main window. Bryce smiled as he parked his car in the spot with the owners sign nailed to a wooden pole. He had some of the best mechanics in New Orleans working for him. With business booming over the past six months, Bryce was able to upgrade many of the shops tools, complete a few decorative projects that made the place look more professional and hire two new mechanics. He even hired an administrative assistant who handled most of the paper work and appointments. Everything in his life was going great. The only thing missing was Mitch. It felt like his heart had been ripped from his chest once he heard the news. Bryce hated the fact that his friend didn't come and talk to him before ending his life. As close as they were there was no doubt that Bryce would've accepted him regardless if he was gay or not. Bryce thought about Mitch quite often and wished he was around to share in his success.

Bryce greeted his workers, then went to shake the hands of each person waiting to get work done on their car. He walked around to make sure that the coffee pots were filled, then put out a fresh box of Dunkin Doughnuts. Bryce checked the bathrooms to make sure they were clean, paper towels and soap dispensers were filled, then headed to his office. If it was one thing he learned, it was that little things made all the difference.

Bryce glanced out of his window and noticed Camille getting out of her 3 series BMW. He quickly left his office to meet her in the waiting area. Camille shot him a small smile as she walked up to the counter.

"What are you doing here?" he asked.

"My car was making some noises and I've heard this is the spot to get good service at a reasonable price," Camille replied.

Bryce smiled. "Well, we try our best. So, what kind of sounds is your car making?"

"How about you ride with me to get a cup of coffee so you can tell me because it's hard to explain," Camille suggested. "But don't be surprised if I choose a place that's on the other side of town though," she flirted.

Bryce was caught completely off guard, but he could

only laugh and nod his head. When the two of them walked out the shop, Camille handed him her keys. Bryce opened the passenger side door to let her in, then walked around to the other side.

"Hey boss, you coming right back!" Jose yelled out.

Bryce looked inside the car at Camille's long legs then back over to the garage. "I doubt it. This might take a while."

Also by J. Tremble

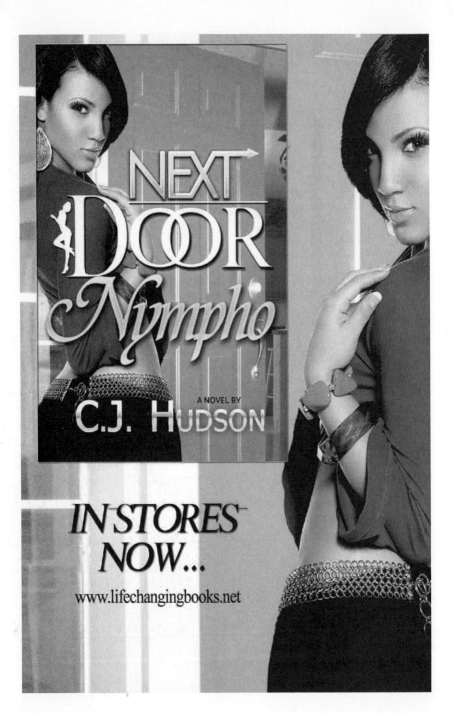